THE KID THAT COULD

This little fiction was self-published under a different title by a pseudonymous author in 1971. I have edited and re-written the original here and there at the urging of my wife, Genie Chipps, founder and proprietor of Chipps & Co, publishers. Genie runs her press from the dining room table. I work in the basement. It is nice to find your publishing house so close to home.

Bill Henderson

The Kid that Could

a novel by

Bill Henderson

Chipps & Co.

© 1990 by Bill Henderson
ISBN 0–916366–62–6
All rights reserved.
Chipps & Co./ Pushcart Press
W. W. Norton & Company
500 Fifth Ave
New York, NY 10110

THE KID THAT COULD

One

ONE day my ex-girl, Mirabella, was off from school with a bad attack of hay fever. Her mom went to a committee meeting and left Mirabella next to the air conditioner.

Mirabella got bored. She packed a lunch box and trotted her basset into the woods for a picnic.

Hours later she was sloshing in the sludge next to a stream—her foot was snagged in a tangle of roots. The basset had deserted her after a rabbit. The sun set beyond Valley Forge and the last of the fireflies drifted into the twilight.

Mirabella's mom had returned about five o'clock. When she hollered upstairs for Mirabella, all that answered was the humming air conditioner. She telephoned her husband's gang; they scurried around with no luck. Mrs. Mason begged for volunteers from the church. Mirabella belonged to the Gardenia Gathering there. I was a Wolf in Echelon Six.

Disguised as an ordinary boy, I was sitting at the kitchen table scooping the peanut butter out of a Skippy jar. I was the first to discover that Skippy's jar was best for fireflying, because it has the widest mouth, and I taught the other kids that. About eight o'clock Reverend Hocheisen called up, frantic because Mirabella had disappeared. Pop whipped me to the church. All the kids from the Echelon and Gardenia Gathering got a password which we shouted to keep in touch. We shined penlites straight up so that helicopters hovering overhead could keep count and radio if we were strung out wrong.

We hunted all night with no luck. Three days later some Pennsylvania State Troopers came up with her lunch box and her basset, but no Mirabella. So they cancelled the hunt.

Of course I didn't give up. On my own I rescued Mirabella! If only I'd been old enough to run for President of the Student Senate! I could have had the election by 5,000 votes to zilch for Hunnicut! All the in-kids would have swung to me, crowning me spiritual dictator of the whole junior high. Any girl would have been mine! If only *People* had noticed me then!

10

I'd have been a pure hero, without all these ridiculous complications. People wouldn't be churning with anxiety and ranting on street corners. Newsmen wouldn't call me dirty names. The neighborhood and the nation would be at peace. I would have rescued a girl. That would have been that. A clean hero, like King Arthur.

As it was then, the Neighborhood Church elected me an honorary Montezuma, the town gave me a huge parade.

Now I sit in my cell. But I'm not allowed to do much.

I'm not allowed to make love to Tania. She left unsparked through the steel door. Today she fitted three Smithsonian Institution fossils into three bars of complexion soap and smuggled the soap past the chief. We huddled around the washstand while I pretended to be scrubbing my pimples.

She had a two million year old lizard fossil and a frog fossil the same age. In the last bar she hid the mutation that sprang from their mating.

We named the third fossil BWFL, for Budding Winged Frog Lizard, since it had sprouted two wingy bone structures at its shoulders. The brain pan of BWFL was three times the size of its parents', which is pretty much when you think about it. Tania said she'd check into that and she promised to do all she could to spring Kathy. Before the chief clanged the door, Tania threw me a goodbye birthday kiss.

Staring at the sealed door, I remembered cooler days, the glorious preview, right after I hauled Mirabella out of that stream.

I saved her life because I was the best fireflyer. Each summer when the fireflies returned to the twilight, the neighborhood kids hunkered in my back yard, waiting until it was dark enough to see the blink and still light enough to make out the silhouette after the blink. Then we all began swishing our Skippy jars in the air.

That year grandpop might have made his first and only getaway from the Golden Age senior citizens home. I was shaking a fly out of the jar into my paper bag when I spied this man creeping up our driveway, wearing rimless glasses, an orange suit with no buttons buttoned and carrying a rough walking stick. It looked exactly like grandpop's disguise. He stood on the lawn and waited while all the kids dashed out of the yard and surrounded him. When he spoke I still thought it might be grandpop, but he'd lost so much weight and his voice cracked.

"Grandpop!" I blurted. The man snorted and tapped me into silence with his stick.

He told us he was making this study of the firefly and we could earn a nickel for each bug we caught and handed over to him. According to all records, he said, the firefly suddenly up and appeared in Utah in the middle of 62,000 B.C.; before that there was no history of anything even like a firefly. He said he wanted to look into that. He also wanted to investigate why it blinked its cold light, and how. Nobody ever really solved that mystery, he said. He wondered if the firefly was attempting to tell us something. Was it trying to lead us somewhere?

He ordered us to collect as many fireflies as we could each evening and staple them in paper bags with our names crayoned on the bags. We should leave the bags at the foot of the whispering willow before midnight. In the morning we'd find the money we had earned in the bag.

Nobody saw the man again, but we all did what he said and a lot of kids stashed away a lot of loot. Soon they had caught most of the fireflies in the area and they began to squabble over the few that came out. Kids bashed into each other, hollered for their dads and there were angry feelings all fall and winter.

I got the brainstorm that I'd make more dough by hunting the deep woods. The night of Mirabella's rescue, late in the season, I was hot on the tail of a firefly that only blinked once in a while and was usually far from where he had blinked before. I figured he was old, and sick of blinking. I trailed him for hours as he flew further and further into the woods, ending up over the muskrat stream, where he didn't budge, hovering over the spot like a star.

I snuck up on him with the Skippy jar ready in the air and on his next blink I winged the jar down. It plopped into the mud. His blinker had lit up the foot of a body! It was Mirabella, unconscious under the root bank. I pried open the roots and toted her through the night to her dad's house. But I couldn't be happy with my parade and honors.

Right after the parade, mom told me that grandpop had died in the Golden Age.

Two

THE last time I had definitely seen grandpop alive was about a year after they committed him to Uncle Charlie's Golden Age.

Mom had promised to stop my allowance and pack me out to a California military school if I ever messed with grandpop again. I risked it and snuck off from elementary school on my bike.

The ride across the Schuylkill to the Golden Age took all morning. I hid my bike in the swampy barrens and ran up a road to a high brick wall where a poster said "Welcome to the Golden Age, the Supreme Reward." It was signed by Uncle Charlie, as proprietor, and pop, as chief engineer.

Since it was the early days and Uncle Charlie was short on dogs and guards, I scrambled over the wall undetected. The land on the other side roasted in the September sun. Heat waves rippled up from the gravel. No trees or bushes, it was solid gravel to the horizon. Ahead of me, flags drooped from the chapel steeple of a village surrounded by a log wall with log towers, like in an old Cisco Kid movie. I tripped on a black tube and some gates flew open. Uncle Charlie's recorded voice drawled "Watch out for them swingin' doors." I stumbled into the deserted village and the doors slammed shut behind me, echoing off the glass dome that covered the whole works.

The cobblestone streets had ruts cut into them, pretending that carriage wheels had rolled over them for centuries, which made running tricky. I jumped on a moving belt sidewalk and jetted through the fort, past an empty barber shoppe, sheriff's office and Ye Olde Ice Cream Parlor. "Grandpop! Grandpop!" I hollered until I had to leap off the belt at the exit gate. A sign said "Leaving Fort Henry, Beware of Wild Dogs and Indians."

Out on the flat gravel land again, I ran into a bunch of sweating savages, Puerto Ricans in red loin cloths and headdresses. "O.K. let's have it

16

again you guys. For two bucks an hour I want you up that wall like you meant it!" a queerly dressed white man shouted at them through a bull horn. The Puerto Ricans scowled and fitted arrows in their bows. "Anybody seen my grandfather?" I asked. The white guy set down his bull horn and turned for me. It was Uncle Charlie, the ex-Broadway actor.

I took off for the next fort, far across the gravel. Uncle Charlie cut in front of me. "Stick 'em up nephew!" he laughed, jabbing a rubber spear at my stomach. I raised my hands. "Name, rank and age?"

"I came to talk over some stuff with grand-pop."

"What sort of 'stuff'?"

"Fireflies . . . personal things that aren't any of your darn beeswax."

Uncle Charlie lowered his spear and shook hands with his hand-buzzer joke. He smiled. "How's it feel to be in the Supreme Reward?"

"I just want to talk to grandpop. Take me there!" I said, rubbing the buzzer welt in my palm.

"You know you're not supposed to be here. Death's not for little kids."

"I am *not* a little kid. I'm ten years old. Now will you take me or not?"

"You know I've never been fond of his nonsense. He's just a client like any other. You've got to be hard-headed about these things."

"I'll find him! You won't stop me with that phony spear either!"

"Maybe you can come along for a tour sort of. . . . Let's run up to the fort and saddle us some Walt Disney jackasses." Uncle Charlie said, hiking up his robes to keep from tripping. Inside the stable I asked "How come you dress like this?"

"It works, Kipper. Reminds clients of their Greek heritage. Remember boy, what works works."

"What works works."

"That's the ticket."

Before I had a chance to ask him what he meant, he had yanked two real, mechanical burros out of the stable. I had trouble balancing but Uncle Charlie relaxed and messed with his lute as he bounced along, explaining the jackasses were his idea, cars were dangerous with so many oldsters around. "I'm up to 2,000 acres and four forts, each fort more perfect than the one before," he said.

In a half-hour we arrived at the banks of a lake with a three-masted sailing boat anchored on it. We sat in the shadows of the burros and ate a lunch of tuna fish sandwiches from Uncle Charlie's saddle bag. In the distance I could make out the peaks of Philadelphia.

"That's the G. A. Nautical Complex; created

that lake in five days by damming the Schuylkill. The boat took ten days to build, an authentic replica of the Mayflower. Each July fourth we stage famous sea battles and if anything goes wrong the rest of the year, we pull up sail and scoot down river," he yukked hysterically.

"I've got to hurry, Uncle Charlie," I said, starting to remount. The burro screamed and bucked around in a circle with his heels flashing at my head. Uncle Charlie collapsed, writhing until his toga was yellow. After pulling himself together, he grabbed the reins and removed a thumbtack from under the saddle. Uncle Charlie had a million practical joke notions, a regular riot.

Outside the walls of the next fort were acres of shuffleboard courts jammed with old men smoking pipes and women knitting, all wearing the official client's toga and large name button, especially necessary in maintaining identity, Uncle Charlie explained. As we passed through corridors of hurrahing shuffleboarders, a blinking light announced we had reached Fort Plymouth Rock, and the doors banged open while trumpets sounded from the towers. Wrinkled men and ladies hurried out waving little fort flags. The music class stood on the moving sidewalk and sang us through the fort. Before leaving, Uncle Charlie dismounted and danced with an old lady. Was I amazed to see it was grandpop's fiancée, the Flower Lady!

I slid down and pulled on her toga, but she was having so many kicks that she wouldn't remember grandpop.

"He loved you!" I yelled after her.

By the time we left, Uncle Charlie and his burro were smothered with flowers.

We reined up a quarter of a mile from the next fort. "It might be dangerous if I got any closer," he said. "Each year I tease a town into official rebellion. Good for the clients, unites 'em against a common enemy. Be careful going in there. First, don't mention my name; second, they're expecting sort of a retaliatory raid. Keep your head down. He's in there somewhere, probably in the stockade or psychiatric service for some fantasy."

He buzzered my hand and headed back to Fort Plymouth Rock chortling, leaving me alone on the plain. From there I couldn't even see old Billy Penn's statue on Philadelphia City Hall. If I knew what I know now I would have hoofed it out of there pronto. But the sky descended to the gravel and it was God's sky and I was God's child, so I booted my burro onward.

All the towers of this fort were occupied by ancient guards peering off at the horizon through binoculars as if they were expecting a very big deal. I shinnied up a log, rolled over the top unseen and landed at the edge of a cement field. At one end of the field, a crowd of old ladies in pink togas, serenaded by an accordionist in a white summer suit, smacked badminton birds. At the other end, the blue-togaed men lambasted ping-pong balls. I hurried over and asked them where I could find grandpop.

Then I saw him, leaning against the leg of a table, chewing on a blade of marsh grass he had miraculously dug out of the gravel. I squatted next to him, but he didn't look at me. He was sketching a firefly in the gravel with his finger. I realized the music had stopped and I didn't hear the socks of the ping-pong balls any more. "Surprise!" I said, reaching out to shake his hand. But he didn't budge. So I took his hand and shook it anyway. Then he looked at me. Nothing was in his eyes!

I asked him how he was and how the food tasted and was it him with the fireflies and how did he escape to collect the firefly bags. But he didn't answer, smiling off at the clouds sweeping high in the atmosphere. Now and then he'd turn and smile at me too, but nothing was in his smile either.

Just as the period ended and the accordionist started a slow number, grandpop glanced at me like he had remembered something. "What was the ocean temperature this summer?" he asked.

"About sixty-five most days. It rained a lot too, but there wasn't any sign of him. I went to the ocean every morning."

Grandpop struggled to his feet, still smiling, and drifted off with the old men, who followed the musician to the town square where they assembled around a fountain of the Angel of Death with wings outstretched and water pouring out of its mouth. There was a sing-along of "Home on the Range" and the nurses stoked up a barbecue and served everybody hot dogs and baked beans. For dessert we roasted marshmallows on wire pokers.

Pillows were handed out and we took a nap around the fountain. "Any word from the King?" grandpop asked with his eyes shut.

Before I could answer, the Indians attacked!

The last I saw of grandpop he was shuffling off into the twilight towards the safety of the chapel while the musicians played "Old Rugged Cross." I thought I heard him holler "Wear the King's color at my funeral!" but I wasn't sure.

Cannons exploded from the towers; old women screamed; air raid sirens went bloop, bloop, bloop. The nurses tried to calm the few clients left in the street but they ran around wildly, holding their heads. I ducked into the Saloon where mobs of people cringed under tables. Three Indians lifted the front window and fired blanks. I ran out the ladies' entrance, not seeing grandpop anywhere. When an Indian hit me with a suction cup arrow, I executed a dramatic death scene on the sidewalk. My tongue lolled, my eyes rolled, my arms clutched my stomach. Still dying, I was transported to the wall. I mounted my mechanical burro and charged for the horizon.

On the way out of the Golden Age, I saw a long line of old folks moving into Fort Henry. It was almost midnight when I got back to my bike and pedaled across the Schuylkill.

Three

I tried to straighten up my mind to be brave for the funeral, but I kept remembering grandpop, about the Schwinn and the flute. I wondered if I'd ever know the commands of the crusade or find out how he died or who killed him.

When I finally showed up downstairs, mom listed the morning schedule: first, breakfast; last, a funeral suit. She was pretty peeved. On the breakfast table, the WAXX radio "wake-up-right" New Order Evangelist (Reverend Hocheisen) was hollering through his Saturday morning show. He prophesied the invasion of the West Coast by hordes from the Orient and a simultaneous earthquake, as predicted in Revelations

11, 13 and confirmed by the stars. Pop spooned his Special K and nodded.

Mom served up a low calorie meal of skim milk, vitamin pills, Tang and a large bowl of oatmeal with sliced peaches. I'll say this for mom, even though she was pretty upset with the way I was developing, she promised "no matter where you end up, your mother won't let you go hungry."

On the dot of eleven, mom revved up the Yugo and honked for me to get a move on; the relatives would be flocking in soon and we didn't have long to find a suit that fit. I was an embarrassing six foot one inch at age twelve. If I'd had Mirabella then to tell me that height made me sexually superior, I might not have been so embarrassed.

The town haberdashery was a yellow brick building with battlements, a sharp idea since kids liked buying in a castle. Flapping banners advertised "low overhead" and "whopping discounts." I remembered to record the castle idea in my diary under "Suggestions on How to Make a Million," as mom and me clomped over the drawbridge into a huge hall with miles of suits. A man with a measuring tape and fake eye patch popped out from behind a rack.

"A boy's suit for general use that would also do for a funeral. Something conservative," mom announced.

"Odd-sized I imagine?" he asked.

"That's right."

"Orange with shoulder pads," I let him know.

Ignoring me, mom selected a dark green suit and the man pointed the way to a dressing room with a barred window. I came back wearing the suit, but it was too small. "If you didn't have such a big rear end," mom said.

I wandered off to a rack of fancy sports coats, unhooked an orange job, and snuck into the dressing room. The man opened the curtain, grabbed it and laid another dark green suit over my shoulder. "That should do it," he commented.

"My grandfather asked me to wear this color to his funeral," I explained. "Orange is the color of Horace, King of Fireflies. He's the God of Music, Light, On-Going, Laughter and other stuff. He defeated the God of Darkness, Death, Depression, Destruction."

But the guy played dense.

"The battle was in 62,051 B.C., autumn in Arkansas. It's been a guerrilla war ever since. Grandpop was a general. He knew the magic words of the crusade, the flyspec."

He yawned and folded my old pants into a paper bag and walked away with mom to select a tie. Snatching another orange number, I broke for the drawbridge in my best cross-country form. He spotted me at the last second and flipped a switch. As the drawbridge neared its apogee, I clawed to the end and toppled into the moat.

I waited in the car until mom arrived with my pants and shoes and the dark green suit. She handed the dripping sports coat to the salesman, informing me I was lucky there weren't any cops outside the castle, otherwise I'd be under arrest for indecent exposure, a permanent record offense, a very horrendous business.

When we pulled into the driveway, the house was roaring with relatives.

Four

O_N mom's orders, I tempted Willy into the woods with a Milk Bone and chained him to the radio tower. When I got back, mom yelled at me to set out an ice bucket of Coke for the relatives, who were sitting in the conversation pit gabbing about diseases and school work and how much cash Uncle Charlie was making in the retirement business. I stuck toothpicks in the miniature hot dogs and set them on the coffee table. I was breaking out card tables for Bridge and Scrabble when somebody thumped on the window. Uncle Charlie peeked over the ledge, wearing a red wig and mirror sun glasses.

Outside I found him standing in a rhododendron bush. He asked me if I'd seen any fuzz lurking. I said I hadn't. "Say, Kipper, show me to the croquet gear. Might as well pick up some change while I'm here."

I walked him to the garage and he gathered the wickets and I carried the balls and mallets. I helped him dig in the wickets.

"Uncle Charlie, tell me something?" I asked, smacking the goal stake with a mallet.

"Name it."

"How'd grandpop die?"

"Content as a lamb. It's in the contract."

"I mean *how* did he. . . . "

"It works like this. At the G. A. nobody passes away alone: they're completely enveloped by a sense of their importance in American history. The togas remind them of their democratic roots in Ancient Greece; the burros are like Jesus rode—a reminder of religious heritage; the architecture recalls the spirit of the Wild West and so do the Indian raids. Living in that heady environment, some of our citizens swoon away."

"They die?"

"We nickname it the Orgasm of History. It's like if you touch a five thousand year old Egyptian pyramid or the Roman Colosseum or Druid Ruins, you get a powerful, indefinable surge, sort of an instant awe of that which is ancient. In

29

the G. A. everything contributes to this surge. That's why every senior citizen has that blank expression."

"Did grandpop get the orgasm? Is that how he was killed?" Uncle Charlie took a practice swing at my feet. "Well what happened?"

"Now calm down. You can be sure your grandfather achieved the Supreme Reward. Like I said, it's guaranteed. How's your croquet form, cous?" he hollered at relatives walking up the path to the kitchen door. Uncle Charlie was a darn good organizer. In a few minutes he had fifteen relatives making bets and bashing one another's balls into the woods.

I retreated into the house and messed with a few Scrabble letters. But I was only a kid; my word power hadn't improved yet.

"Wasn't that a fine funeral. Except his mouth was sewn down a little tight at the corners," Reverend Hocheisen said, taking a seat.

"What funeral?" I asked.

Aunt Anna and Uncle Bob arrived and we let them play too. Reverend Hocheisen's word power was so well developed that he led by a lot of points when pop came over. "Excuse me. I'm taping for the final generation. Would you all please say a word to put the occasion on record," pop said quietly.

"The cat's got my tongue," Aunt Anna giggled.

"Please try."

"Hello there futureland, whatever you may be, be good," Aunt Anna laughed.

"Thank you, Anna. Next is Uncle Bob, my wife's brother," pop said, pointing the microphone.

"We're all at a funeral. Does anybody die any more where you are?" Uncle Bob asked.

"Reverend Hocheisen, pastor of the Neighborhood Church," pop announced. Unfortunately the wire caught on the corner of the board and messed up the words Reverend Hocheisen had fitted together. He lost the game later when Uncle Bob remembered an unusual Army word with "z" on triple letter score.

"I'm a minister of the gospel and somebody just fouled up my Scrabble game," Reverend Hocheisen said peevishly. On second thought he added, "I'm founding the New Order, joining sports, ESP, astrology, sociology, culture and ritual sacrifice from all lands and times. I hope it is working out for you."

By mistake, Reverend Hocheisen passed the mike to me. I managed to blurt "did anybody find out if my grandfather got the orgasm of history?" before pop pressed the button that erased my voice.

I counter-attacked out back. I watched Uncle Charlie clunking the croquet ball around. He'd won seventy dollars so far and nobody had offered any competition except his girl. Then she discovered he'd slipped in loaded balls. Everybody walked away mumbling.

"You can play chess with me," I said, hoping to trap him into a murder confession.

"Sure, Kipper," he agreed. He fitted his girl's ten spot into his billfold.

He beat me in the first game and won fifty cents. He refused to even mention grandpop. Halfway through our second game, his girl stalked into the room and glared out the glass. "Don't be a sore loser, fruit drop," he called. She stiffened.

Uncle Charlie's chin snapped to his chest and his laugh silenced the whole house full of relatives. Starting as a tuba, it climbed from A to G, shifted into the next octave, became a clarinet, climbed from A to G, switched to a piccolo and soared out of ear range. It seemed exactly planned, like a player piano.

His girl's head jerked down to her chest. Her eyes first pleaded, then misted. Her head fell back with his until her soft throat was bared to the ceiling and you could see right up her nose. Her long legs buckled, her body turned to syrup. She lurched laughing across the living room onto his lap.

"Your move, Kipper."

"How'd you do that?"

"Take your knight?"

"No. Make up with your girl?"

"It's a secret laugh. All part of the universal secret, What Works Works."

"I don't get it. Could you teach me?"

"Someday you'll catch on."

He trapped my darn queen in his next move, so I handed him the rest of my allowance for the week.

Billy, the maid, rang the brass dinner bell. "It's cake and ice cream time, cake and ice cream!" she yelled. The relatives filed in and sat on the chairs and floors while Uncle Charlie pulled his wig over his eyes and contacted the Golden Age on his tie clip phone. Billy closed the Venetian blinds to set the mood for pop's grace: "I wish the Lamb of the Lord would come soon and wash the world whiter than snow."

"Amen," the relatives responded.

"You shouldn't of said the wish out loud," Billy commented.

"Billy hush, and get the refreshments," mom said.

Billy snorted through the kitchen door.

After we finished our refreshments, pop opened the Family Bible to Ecclesiastes and read "Wine is a mocker, strong drink is raging and whosoever is deceived thereby is not wise."

"That's what we're chiseling on his headstone," Uncle Charlie chuckled like a conniver.

"Kipper, with all of us assembled in this rare moment, we'd like you to take a simple pledge. Your family wants assurance that you won't follow in the steps of your grandfather. Please read the pledge, sign it, never forget it," mom spoke up, handing me a parchment and pen.

"I, the undersigned child of God, do hereby promise to refrain from alcoholic beverages and to encourage others to keep a sober head, so help me Jesus," I read as my refreshments rose in my throat. I tried to exit for the toilet but tripped on the piano leg. Mom pointed her finger down at me. "You *used* to be a Christian gentleman! This firefly insanity has ruined you!"

"Peg, don't. It's not that important," pop intervened, cradling my head. "Are you o.k., son?"

"Charlie! The heat!" Uncle Charlie's girl screeched.

Mom hustled to the window. Pop snatched up his briefcase and overcoat from the hall closet and galloped for the back door where Uncle Charlie had already disappeared.

Out the front window I saw three cops maneuvering around the Dobermans. One made it and charged up the flagstones. I ran for the den and climbed out a window.

A gold helicopter settled in the back yard while a rope ladder dangled out and Uncle Charlie and pop climbed up it. I rescued the

the wig Uncle Charlie dropped and walked back into the house. Trapped in the kitchen, mom complained "I'm only a stockholder. What do I know?"

Five

I double-timed the steps to Kathy's room, nudged over the cat and lay down holding Kathy's hand. We used to do this all the time for protection, but mom wouldn't let me any more since she said I was too old. I slipped a pillow under our heads and tugged the quilt to our chins.

The next thing I knew mom was charging up the stairs: "Get into that suit and shine your shoes!" It took her two minutes to brush Kathy's hair and pull on her little dress and carry her downstairs. Reverend Hocheisen sat all morose at the Scrabble table as she swished past with a veiled face, snapping her fingers.

The Neighborhood Church of the New Order was almost empty. Most of the relatives had started for home after the games because they didn't dig grandpop. I have very crummy relatives, but at least I only see them at funerals. We sat on metal folding chairs in the front row while grandpop reclined in his toga looking furious, as if his eyes might snap open any minute and scare the cake and ice cream out of the rest of them.

The door at the side of the altar opened and closed. I saw the dancer's dress. Mom checked her watch and tapped her toes while relatives behind us talked about getting caught in heavy turnpike traffic. When the recorded guitar music began, mom relaxed and stopped tapping. Reverend Hocheisen hurried out of the side door zipping up his favorite Mayan funeral robe. He nodded at grandpop, clicked on the lamp and read a prayer. "Dear Holy Spirit, we have assembled here today to join this man and. . . . " The lamp flickered off and on. There were long pauses when he couldn't see the paper. I was sure I saw grandpop smile.

Reverend Hocheisen gave up on the prayer and ad-libbed, "In these bewildering times, one seldom meets anybody who is perfect. The man who lies here before us in eternal slumber was a creature of imagination, a fellow who loved inventions and poetry. He goes to the place reserved for all such characters, and if in some ways he may have fallen. . . . " The light shut down for good. I heard a lot of footsteps trooping out behind. "For we are sinners all anyway," Reverend Hocheisen concluded. He clapped three times.

A ballet dancer stepped out timidly—St. George, a goofy girl from school. She wore a ruffled dress and ballet slippers and she had twined funeral flowers in her hair. She waited until Reverend Hocheisen remembered to turn on the *Pathetique Symphony* and announce "St. George will dance 'The Blues' to God's glory and will soon appear on nationwide TV. Check your local listings"; then she leapt and spun in front of grandpop, picking flowers off his stomach and chucking them in the air, giving the dance everything she had—I will admit she tried. But the symphony lasted awful long and I heard more relatives walking out. Finally she wrapped it up and bowed to grandpop.

"To conclude, the deceased had one last wish, that we play a farewell poem, composed and recited by himself. This tape was made a few days ago, I'm told by his grandson, Kip, who is in charge of it," Reverend Hocheisen said.

I walked to the altar and threaded the tape, which had arrived mysteriously by special delivery the day before. It was shocking to hear grandpop's voice. It quavered and squeaked sometimes. When it did, grandpop blew up.

"My last work!" he yelled. "Composed at the Golden Age Death House, a day before Orgasm of History Therapy!" A bottle smashed in the background. "Dedicated to my sons. To be broadcast at my funeral. All praise to Horace, God of Light, Laughter and On-Going; enemy of Death and Depression.

> "There once was a soul
> ninety-three
> Who forgot how it's proper to
> pee. . . . "

The rest of the relatives disappeared out the exits. I swear to God I saw grandpop start to struggle from his coffin! Reverend Hocheisen slammed the lid and sat on it all the way to the cemetery.

Mom figured grandpop needed a whole 1776 log cabin. When we arrived at the G. A. cemetery, the front of the cabin was swung open to shelter the immediate family during services.

One of the pallbearers unrolled a mat of bullrushes to the grave while another one hummed up from the hearse in an electric cart with the coffin on fork lifts. Mom, Kathy and me got in position behind the cart. The gold-helmeted leader grabbed the steering handle and each G. A. pallbearer put a hand on the lid. We marched over the rushes to the cabin.

The leader jerked the handle to the side so that grandpop could be placed on the grave jack, but the cart wouldn't stop. It rolled along into the graveyard. The leader heaved his helmet at grandpop. It clanged hopelessly off the lid.

Grandpop hummed across the cemetery trailing streams of flowers and sympathy cards, colliding with headstones, skidding across somebody's new grave and turning for us. "A blasphemer to the end," mom mumbled as we huddled inside the cabin, waiting.

A wind blew up and firefly clouds scurried over the horizon. Mom made a break for it. In a mad crash, the plaster logs gave way and grandpop plowed into the cabin. We dove outside.

The coffin hit the jack and fell half off, dragging around, smacking the walls until the cabin collapsed in an explosion of plaster dust.

Reverend Hocheisen and the men cleared away some of the ruins and lifted grandpop onto the jack. As the service started, it began to hail. I covered Kathy with bullrushes.

Reverend Hocheisen read a bit from Ecclesiastes about there is a time for everything. Then a part of a poem by Housman, "All the light-footed lads and lilting girls. . . . " He snapped the book shut. "If any man knows any reason why this man and this earth should not be joined, let him dare to step forward or forever hold his peace."

"Hold it!" I said, handing Kathy to mom.

I unpacked my trombone and clamped it together. I managed to get the first note of the Firefly National Anthem right and the second, which is the same as the first by the way, and the next three; but the sixth note was high and I muffed it because of the cold mouthpiece.

Warming the piece in my hand, I decided I was going to play this perfect if it took all year. Out of the corner of my eye I saw the Golden Age jokers pile into the hearse and drive off. The hail was bouncing off my trombone and melting through my suit. Pellets poured down my face with the sweat. After I muffed the second try, mom, Kathy and Reverend Hocheisen retired to the car, waving through the closed windows for me to get a move on.

I looked to the grave. Grandpop was still above ground. I wished he'd yell the magic words to me so I could finish this darn Anthem.

In a little while, the mouthpiece was warming up and so was my lip. I had to make it right before my lip muscles quit on me.

In seven tries I hit it perfect.

I laid my trombone on the coffin, saluted with my arms straight out like wings, and bent down to the coffin. "Let me know what tunes old winker likes," I whispered. I flipped the switch and watched the coffin whir into the grave. "I'll write," I promised, choking.

I tapped on the window and made Reverend Hocheisen power it down. "A few questions," I said.

"Well?"

"Kipper, we're leaving," mom warned.

"Clear up for me what you said in that prayer about grandpop being a sinner. Everybody sins sometimes but that doesn't make them a sinner. Only thieves and murderers are."

"Sunday School's the proper place for this, young man. You should have learned already that sin stems from Martin Luther in the fifteenth century. Good is rewarded; evil, as we have seen in the case of your grandfather, is not."

"The fifteenth century! What use is that!" I said, getting very hot about his casual air.

"Before him even, from Adam and Eve. All men thereafter, you and I too, are sinners. Now Kip, please calm down and join us in the car."

"You mean there's no way out of it!"

"I'm afraid not," he smiled.

"I'll never buy that!" I hollered as he buzzed up the window.

Sinking down in the cold gravel, I wept.

From that day on I thought there really wasn't any way out of it.

The Neighborhood Church re-educated me about sin. I remembered I lived in sin, but should try not to. If I tried hard enough to escape what I had to be, my cup would run over.

Six

ON the Big Day, Tania whammed her fists on my door and yelled to the chief to get a move on with the keys. The chief padded up the hall in his muff muff slippers, cursing to himself. As mayoralty candidate for the Old Way, he didn't figure 6:30 a.m. was any hour for girls to be visiting boys. "Five minutes, young lady; five minutes and then you vamoose!"

"Hurry up, will you!" Tania hollered. She barged into my cell as I threw a blanket around my jockey shorts. "Good morning! Good, good morning!" she greeted me with a lick and a smooch.

I looked her over. She wore her usual day-glo body paint, her MIT Anthropology Department t-shirt and fisherman's rope-soled sandals from the dig near Alexandria. Her red hair whipped all over, but her pencil was firmly in place, as usual, behind her ear. "What've you got there?" I asked.

"A secret."

"Complexion soap?"

"Guess what! Daddy commissioned you Oceanaut Second Class. You're diving to the center of the earth through the Michaelmas fissure!"

I started to tell her she'd done a crummy job, but forgot about it when I saw her eyes. Her arms were still behind her back.

"How come chiefy won't let me stay?"

"He thinks you take advantage of him with the fossils you smuggle in here. It's o.k. He's just a little grumpy; assassination jitters. Come on Tania, what's the secret?"

She hummed a tune and rocked her head, playing cute.

"Tania!"

"Daddy also said you can be a cabin boy in the space voyage to Taurus next year, if you want."

"Big deal. What's behind you?"

"Force me!" she said, backing against the concrete.

"Tania, I just woke up. Now what is it?"

"Voilà!" she hopped around waving it over her head, cartwheeling around the tube, jumping on the couch, throwing her feet out and breaking the darn leg when she landed. "Fresh off the press!" she hollered. "It's the first one printed!"

It was the copy of *People*! My face was on the cover! Months of planning, searching and just plain hard work had finally paid off!

Tania bugged me all the same. That was my dance! She stole my celebration! What did she know about troubles, the President's daughter? What did she know about being hunted down by a whole army, about pimples and a big nose and growing tall as the Washington Monument? What did she know about starting as a boy hero and then being laughed at by the in-crowd and never giving up until you made it to the top of history, pimples or no pimples, monument or no monument?

I thought about splitting up with her, but *People* got me involved. I flipped through the article, headlined "Kip, The First Rung Up."

The photos were from pop's Family Archives. He kept most of his records about me there, including hand and foot casts I made in kindergarten, tapes of my birthday parties and lots of snapshots. Also stored there were records of ancestors with birth, death and marriage certificates back to the Civil War; at least that's what pop said.

The large picture under the headline, captioned "in happier days," was of Reverend Hocheisen, mom, pop and me on our driveway. Reverend Hocheisen had just launched his big evangelistic campaign in a tent. Pop sat on his new leaf mulcher, which he had been showing off to Reverend Hocheisen. He wore his combat boots because our neighbor, Mr. Pentapholis, had just sliced off two toes in his mulcher, which pop said was because Mr. Pentapholis divorced his wife. Since nobody is without sin, pop wanted to make sure he didn't lose any of *his* toes. Reverend Hocheisen stood beside me grinning like a maniac, his hand weighing down my head with red stone rings.

Just before the picture was taken he had told me I was his Ultimate Heir to leadership of the New Order. And I was only nine years old!

After dinner, Reverend Hocheisen had leaned back, and told us what he said was a true story called "The Man Who Forgot to Tithe." One day The Man Who Forgot to Tithe saw a Jaguar sports car he dug and made a down payment on the spot. Soon he was wearing ascots and a toupee and spending weekends messing in New York. He fell behind in his car payments and to make up for it, he quit tithing. He got another loan for a thirty foot cabin cruiser. The next time he prayed, he found out God wasn't listening. So he sold his boat and toupee; but still God wouldn't tune in. The man began going to women. God wouldn't give him one ear. When he turned to liquor, God shut him off for good. The man ended up driving his Jaguar off a bridge in a last ditch attempt to get God to pay attention.

Reverend Hocheisen said it was sad. He led us in prayer while we held hands around the table. Later, pop wrote out a check for a thousand dollars to the New Order. He was named a co-founder.

Reverend Hocheisen hustled off to his tent in the city.

For the highlight of the evening, he presented me on stage with my Sunday School attendance pins, the longest chain in the state, dangling from my lapel into my pants pocket. He described me as "a paradigm example to the youth of the world" and attached an Inca Anklet, his highest award, to my ankle. Then he made the public announcement of the Ultimate Heir business.

The audience stood and sang "Red and Yellow, Black and White, They Are Precious in His Sight, Jesus Loves the Little Children of the World." I must admit I was darn egotistical about it all.

Pop was sitting with Kathy and mom on the stage. During the singing, Kathy woke up and pop was sure she'd been cured. He stood ram-rod straight for the rest of the service in tribute to the Holy Ghost. When Kathy fell into the trance again during the Benediction, pop had a hard time explaining.

All my life I had heard a lot about God, Jesus and the Holy Ghost from pop. He knew things other pops didn't know. He told me the end of the world was due on Jesus' birthday, as promised in the Bible. After the last Chinese H-bomb had exploded and all the sinners had been burnt up, the Holy Ghost would come again and take us to his bosom.

I asked pop if people who mulched their lawn on Sundays like Mr. Pentapholis would be burned. "Unless you or me can save him. I've done everything I know how," he sighed.

Pop had reasons to believe that our family had received a Call. He pointed to miracles like Kathy's sickness to keep us humble before God; like Uncle Charlie's success with old age homes that gave pop a good job and kept the family in loot. Like him being named a co-founder of the New Order and me the Ultimate Heir.

Pop counted on me to pick up the mission when he got too old or died.

In another *People* photo I was only eight years old. I posed beside pop's three-legged Felt

Board in my Arab robe, gazing mystically off at the sky. A crowd of little jokers gathered around on sleds and giggled into pop's camera. The kids that memorized Bible verses held up the Tootsies I gave them.

David and Goliath was their favorite story. They had flocked in with their cowboy outfits and atomic grenade launchers until it looked like some sort of army in my backyard. For openers I asked them to give testimonials about their brothers fighting the enemy. One boy's brother was tortured; another told how the enemy burned churches; the last was from a little girl whose brother lost his arms and legs.

My sermon on David and Goliath was packed with an important message for the kids. David, a boy of God, was also a soldier, like their brothers. I told the kids to pretend they were David's army watching the battle from a hillside. Pop had cut out a felt Goliath ten times bigger than David, as big as some of the little kids. But David was so tiny that the kids in the back complained they couldn't see him. "Go, go Goliath!" a wise bully yelled.

The message was that Goliath was a Philistine. There was nothing worse in those days, I taught. Indicating David with pop's pointer, I said he was a good kid who obeyed his parents, picked up his toys and stuff, and did good in school. "Now watch what happens to Goliath when he meets God's boy!"

I ducked behind the board, nodding the go ahead to Larry Hunter who could knock a crow out of the sky with a marble and his slingshot. He bull's-eyed Goliath with a raw egg that unfortunately splattered over the kids in the front row. I got heck from their moms later. "That's what God wants done to evil people!" I proclaimed, raising my hands in a V for victory salute. The kids cheered and threw their scarves and mittens in the air. The guy who rooted for Goliath was stoned with ice balls. They cheered even more when mom carted out the hot cocoa and doughnuts.

After they had sledded home, a little girl handed me her pet hamster, which was shaking and couldn't move its rear legs. "You're too young for healings," pop intervened, handing the hamster back to the girl. Pop may have been pretty emotional about his religion but he sure plotted my career carefully.

There were other pictures inside *People,* including one of me chatting with the President this year and him leaning forward in his rocker to make a point, and one of grandpop and me posing with our bicycle.

But the most important picture was the cover shot, the one pop liked to call my official portrait.

It was taken by him after he had decided I proved myself with the Felt Board and was ready for Communion. It was the summer after my ninth birthday. I was standing in front of Reverend Hocheisen in my dark red Communion robe, my eyes wide and far away, my head back, the Aztec Temple Mug at my lips, the first blood flowing down my throat. In my mind was this vision of a little girl's panties I saw floating from a clothes-line that morning.

I'd made it through the broken body alright, but when Reverend Hocheisen bent down to pour the blood in the mug, the vision of the pant-ies reared up. He turned to me smiling, holding the mug out.

The harder I fought the vision, the dirtier it got. Once I forced my mind to be empty and pure but the sweat dribbled off my armpit and down my side and the vision flashed back. I started to tell him I really shouldn't try it because I had this vision, but he shut my mouth with his fixed-on Baptism, Communion, Marriage smile.

I banished it for a second time by concen-trating on his teeth. Splash, the sweat dripped and the panties flowed from the clothesline. I mumbled "I can't, really," turning to mom beside me. She was smiling. I tried pop on the other side but he was smiling. I looked for help some-where in the congregation behind me. Row after row of teeth.

As I lifted the mug and pop raised his flash, I prayed desperately to the Holy Ghost to erase the vision. My hands and the mug were trembling. It showed up in the photo as blurs. The blood I spilled was just beginning to trickle out of the corner of my mouth while the rest rushed down my throat and the panties blew off the line.

I knew the Holy Ghost was going to get me for that and I was grateful he didn't torture me by postponement. I figured it was a pretty good example of the mercy of H. G. On Monday I was paddling around Lake Sunshine with the other kids from Camp New Order Word-O'-Life, further out than the rest, having a fine time in my old inner tube. Chris, the lifeguard, was messing with his girl and didn't see me or he would have blown me back in.

The sun was warm, the waves rippled by. I felt safe.

Then the water suddenly chilled, me hoping it was just a cold spot in the lake. The sun disappeared under an enormous black cloud; whitecaps jumped all around me. It was time! I tried to paddle to shore, but the icy wind blew me further out. A shape leaped out of the water at me, swosh, right out and in again. H. G.! Disguised as a white duck!

"Chris, Chris!" I screamed, paddling as fast as I could move my hands. The duck flashed high out of the lake, while I screamed in general. I saw Chris hop from his stand and run to the water's edge, holding his girl's hand, taking his darn time about it. Swish, Splash! H. G. jumped at me. I was soaking and cold from His waves. I paddled; H. G. leaped.

I paddled too hard and turned over, my head jamming against the pebbles on the bottom, my feet pointing through the tube at the black cloud. H. G. was killing me upside down like St. Peter; quite an honor I figured.

Running out of air, I ripped through the Lord's Prayer and reviewed the nine years of my life. I felt pretty good, going to be with my Heavenly Dad.

Chris' darn girl friend pulled me out by the heels, threw me over her shoulder and trucked me back to the beach where she applied artificial respiration. When I came to my lips were smeared with pink lipstick and Chris stood over me, hands on hips, yukking as if he'd never dug anything as hilarious as a drowning kid with his feet in the air.

I was so embarrassed I quit Camp Word-O'-Life. I told pop I didn't want to waste my summer in idle play: I wanted to read the Bible all the way through a couple of times instead. That turned him on. He upped my allowance fifty cents and let me go to three Walt Disney re-runs. He saw a great career as Ultimate Heir ahead of me.

He promised me that soon I could try my hand at faith healing. But I didn't get a chance until junior high. And then it was a human being, not a hamster.

Seven

Amonth after I saved Mirabella in the stream, she came down with a thing called Ichthyosaurus, a rare, evolutionary disease, and was quarantined in her house.

Mirabella had always been a New Order church-going kid with a laughing smile and long light hair and frilly dresses with polka-dot bows. Since we were little we took picnics together or baked mud pies or piled up snow forts. She was about the best friend I had back then. She used to make me feel good just seeing her ride down the sidewalk on her pink bicycle with the noise-making balloons. I thought it was worse than anything when she was locked away.

I remember all her Venetian blinds shut tight and her only visitors every day, her doctor and tutor. I remember her father arrested for dynamiting the muskrat stream. None of the kids heard any news of Mirabella after that and most forgot about her disease—except St. George. She said Mirabella's disease was proof of Siva's Second Coming in the U.S.A.

During those months, I tried to uncover the exact reason why Mirabella got sick. I didn't know of any big sins she had sinned.

A couple of times I went and rang their doorbell, but they never answered.

One day in seventh grade, our teacher clapped and announced we were going to get a new pupil who we might not recognize. She said we should all treat her kindly since she had this chronic disease. Her mother appeared in the glass and knocked unhappily. When the teacher opened the door, a chauffeur pushed Mirabella in on a wheelchair.

The kids shrieked. Even sitting down Mirabella was taller than anybody in the seventh grade. Her short, half-gray half-black hair had fallen out at the crown and her face was as pale as an onion. We agreed in whispers that she had died on the way up the hall and her mother, who was busy signing official papers, hadn't noticed it yet.

I chanced a wave like I was scratching my

head. Mirabella waved back! She hoisted her right hand with the help of her left and wiggled her fingers. We saw through her hand; it was as thin as the wing of a flying fish!

When the chauffeur helped Mirabella settle behind her desk, her dress hiked up from her knit stockings and we saw the Ichthyosaurus! The skin on her legs had turned to scales!

Mirabella was allowed out of her wheelchair to exercise for only ten minutes a day since the toes on her feet were growing together and it was painful for her to walk. It was up to a committee of boys, which the teacher appointed when nobody volunteered, to drive Mirabella around whenever the classes changed. The teacher put me at the head of the committee, acting as if it were some big deal. Mirabella suggested my name since I saved her life.

My job lasted only until graduation from seventh grade. In eighth grade she was fitted with special shoes that kept her toes apart so she could hobble for short distances with the aid of two canes. But I still had to escort her since she had thinned out over the summer and was in constant danger of collapsing outright. She was so skinny that with the light behind her I could see her internal organs like a guppy's.

Most days Mirabella lay back in her desk too weak to move anything but her lungs. She had developed a gurgle and sitting two desks from her, I couldn't hear the darn teacher. I begged for a change of seat, but the teacher clamped her hand on my shoulder and frowned "No, Kipper. You're all she has."

I decided it was now or never for my first faith healing. I escorted her to a basement broom closet and asked her if she truly believed. She didn't seem to understand so, since I heard footsteps down the hall, I grabbed her head and whispered "Heal! Heal!" She grabbed me back and cried "Kipper, you're the only one who cares!" At that point the janitor flipped open the closet door and I had to pay him fifty cents to keep it quiet.

On the last day before Thanksgiving vacation, it rained in gallons. I was helping her into her father's black Lincoln when I noticed these two narrow slits in her neck, opening and closing as if gasping for air. I slammed the door and hoofed it for the boys' room. "God Almighty," I groaned, holding my head over the toilet, "what awful sin did she commit?"

Our eighth grade teacher, a nice old lady named Mrs. Littles, delivered another speech about Mirabella. "Students, your dear classmate, Mirabella, is not expected to live out this year. Let's make her last days happy ones; treat her with kindness; shield her from thoughtless children in other grades. See past Mirabella's disease to the nice person she is underneath. Remember, Mirabella's condition is not her fault."

I shot up my hand but Mrs. Littles suddenly dismissed us for recess. I wondered if she had some inside info on whose fault the disease was. I hustled up to her, but before I could open my mouth she looked me straight in the eyes and informed me that this year, since we would learn the social graces in Friday night dancing class, we were expected to take into consideration every member of the grade.

"Mrs. Littles, whatdya mean it's not her fault? Whose fault is it then? Diseases don't just *happen* you know."

"Go out and exercise," she said, turning away.

That Friday night Mrs. Littles walked me aside and told me since I'd sprouted to six feet seven, I was Mirabella's steady dancing partner. "Hey wait a second," I started. But she reminded me I was borderline pass or fail in her U.S. History course.

Mirabella sealed the deal a few minutes later when she presented me with her own home ec. chocolate cake decorated with "To My Favorite Swinger" in wavy icing.

Whenever it was ladies' choice, the girls jumped up at the other end of the gym and barreled towards the guys. In the rear, over-towering all the girls, was transparent Mirabella, tottering straight for me. Sometimes she didn't even *arrive* until the dance was half over. She'd nudge my shoulder with her cane as I sat alone, holding my head in the row of chairs.

When it was men's choice, the in-girls acted as if *I* was the one with Ichthyosaurus. "Don't be a cheater, Kipper. You're Mirabella's boy," they laughed.

As a reward for being Mirabella's boy, Mrs. Littles suggested that the Ladies' Christian Parents Club name me "Christian Youth of the Year." Col. Cole, principal of the junior high, held an award ceremony and gave me the plaque in front of the whole school. Mom nailed it over my bed.

Mirabella's looks really nose-dived during the eighth grade. Since I held her in my arms every Friday, I had a microscopic view of her evolutionary events. Her upper teeth had bucked out almost over her chin. Larry Hunter said they reminded him of the teeth on a dead Mako shark he'd seen on a fishing boat that summer. Even a string of braces that looked more like the anchor chain on an ocean liner did nothing to hold them back in her mouth. Her chin was practically not even there. It was receding as her teeth bucked out.

Above her teeth Mirabella grew a tiny grey mustache that looked like loads of catfish feelers. Filtering through was breath that would have disgusted a swamp. On rainy days, in addition to her gurgle, she hiccupped in a kind of a croak, like a beached blowfish. Finally, she croaked and gurgled so loud that she had to be kicked out of class on wet days and listen at home over a tele-phone hook-up.

This year the scales were evolving up over her torso and down her arms and she was wear-ing metal gloves to keep her fingers from growing together. The rumor went around that she'd been found in the girls' room with her head and neck submerged in the washstand for fifteen minutes.

The other rumor was that I loved MIrabella. The in-kids made up jingles about us because we danced together. Each morning some wise in-kid would greet me with "how's fishing?" They carved our initials in desk tops and crayoned the hall walls with "Kipper and the Mackerel."

Mirabella believed their jokes. As she wrig-gled closer to death, she burned up all her ener-gies in loving me. Every day she snuck a message to me in handwriting so feeble that I couldn't even figure what she was trying to tell me; plus the writing looked more like ocean waves than any human alphabet. But at the end of each note she printed, "I love you too, The Fish."

Mirabella's messages proved to the in-kids that their rumors were true. They said I was in love with Mirabella because I was too giraffe-ish and big-nosed and generally hard up to get any healthy girl interested in me. I was never invited to parties. On party nights, she telephoned me and insisted on trying to spout love words over gurgles and between croaks.

I was sure God wasn't persecuting me for some sin. "Maybe He's grooming me to be another Job," I figured.

As the last days of eighth grade closed in, Mirabella's condition got worse. She never budged from her wheelchair and even her "I love you too, The Fish" was getting sort of wavy. On advancement night, my name was called and I stood up to receive my final report card from Col. Cole. Mirabella heaved herself from her wheelchair and hung on my neck sobbing.

After that the in-girls wouldn't speak to me since they said I must have mistreated Mirabella to make her cry so horribly and I was worse than a beast to do that to a dying girl. One of the pretty ones slapped me at the advancement buffet the next afternoon. The in-girls convinced the in-guys that it was best to leave me by my miserable self. I ate the buffet standing alone in the middle of the cafeteria next to her empty wheelchair.

Meanwhile, Mirabella's father was making a last ditch attempt to cure her Ichthyosaurus. I tore up letters from New Mexico, Idaho, Utah, Oregon and North Dakota. All summer she telephoned long distance to up-date me on the progress she was supposed to be making and to let me know how much she still loved me.

I sent her a registered letter over pop's signature that said I'd been killed in a car crash. But she didn't buy it since the postcards, letters and calls kept pouring in. I answered the phone with "City Zoo." If it was long distance calling I groaned like a camel and hung up.

In the summer before ninth grade, I made up my mind to erase what Mirabella had done to my popularity. I'd soar so high she'd never touch me. I thought up the Virtue Chart. In the first weeks of ninth grade I revved it up and waited for results.

The first result was that mail and calls stopped completely. Some of the in-kids were forgetting I'd been rumored to be in love with a fish.

Then I got an airmail special delivery from Wolfschanze, North Dakota.

"Dear Kipper,

I wonder if you'd do me a favor. Tell the guys and gals that the plastic surgeons and transplant experts have fixed me up. I'll be back to school in a jiffy. See you then.

Mirabella."

Eight

THANKS to the Virtue Chart, I was taking giant steps in popularity. But the day before Mirabella came back I really tasted it in the ninth grade tower.

That's the tower they were tearing down, since they ripped out the guts of the other two towers in the past two years. There's the brand new eighth grade tower with the giant statue of Abe Lincoln reading a book on the roof, and the seventh grade tower with Babe Ruth swinging a bat. Each year they rip out the insides of a tower, starting at the bottom and going up floor by floor, remodeling in a flash so that classes can continue while they work. They bust their way right on up through the roof and add on more floors to keep up with the enrollment explosion. The ninth grade tower, which used to be just two stories, will be forty-two stories this year, topped by F. D. R., the tallest of all.

This year the architects discovered an engineering principle that lets them curve a building to one side, symbolic of the march to the future. Soon all the towers will march to the same side and we will be more famous than Pisa.

But the tearing down and building up made it confusing to get to classes.

On the day before Mirabella's grand entrance, Col. Cole tweeted his whistle and I dashed toward geography in the basement. The workers had been banging around down there for weeks and had already installed the music and air conditioning and had knocked out the stairs to make room for local and express elevators. To get into the basement, the guys used a wood ladder hanging in a hole dynamited through the ceiling. At first the girls used the ladder too, but Shop L guys peeped up their dresses. Col. Cole ordered a temporary elevator.

I was the first to the hole.

A worker leaned on his hydraulic drill singing La Cucaracha. A Grey Area scampered by with his transistor tuned full blast to the World Series. There was the growing roar of hundreds of kids driving for the hole, punching and kicking. Turning backwards, I felt for the first rung. I had made it down a few rungs when the ladder began to wobble. There was Hunnicut at the bottom with a kitchen knife, climbing for me, corkscrewing the knife over his head. "Your sin!" I thought he yelled. Even as the biggest fellow in the school I wasn't going to take on a knife. I dropped my books on his head and sprang out of the hole like a seven foot cricket.

I was trapped by the swarming boys. Whirling, I expected to see Hunnicut attacking. But the hole was empty. "Maybe I'm dreaming things," I thought. "He doesn't have any moral reason to get me."

I snuck back to the hole and dangled my book belt over the edge. I threw a tile down. "Move it!" "Get goin' buddy roll, we'll be late!" they hollered. Col. Cole didn't like it if your foot wasn't past the threshold by his late whistle. Risking it, I stuck my head over the edge of the hole. My books were in a pile at the bottom of the ladder, but no Hunnicut. Some kid put his heel on my rear and shoved me into the hole head first. It's a good thing my biceps were well developed; I caught myself upside down on the last rung and saved a fractured skull.

I scooped up my books and made it just in time to geography. "Fear not those that kill the body, but those that kill the soul," I remembered, calming down to the music and trying to think of what sin.

I didn't see swarthy Hunnicut for another week. He was practicing beach ball catching with the other lunatics, far across the athletic field on a misty morning. He seemed oblivious to the misery he caused me.

That idiot's attack helped ruin my chart rating for the day. The Virtue Chart was my record for God. Of course I couldn't expect Hunnicut to know about things like that.

My main goal, besides ditching Mirabella, was to appear on the cover of *People*. I figured my eighteenth birthday was a good deadline. I chose *People* because it had the most photos of people on the front.

Other goals included curing my pimples. Job beat his boils by maintaining a good record with God and never flying off the handle no matter how raw a deal he got. I mean H. G. took his cows and women and kids and the whole works. But he never flinched. In another word, Patient.

I got my other virtues from Diogenes, Helen Keller, General Ike, Uncle Charlie, Plato, Babe Ruth, pop, Winston Churchill, Pericles, Senator Henry Clay, Mick Jagger, Isaac Newton, Hannibal, Oliver North, Alexander the Great, Col. Cole, and Reverend Hocheisen.

I selected their recommendations from, and hereby give credit to *Presbyterian Life, Sunday Inquirer, Reader's Digest, The Upper Room, T.V. Guide, Time, The Sunday School Times, Boy's Life,* a T.V. movie I forgot the name of, Neighborhood Church, and the dinner table.

The virtues on the chart were:

Aggressive	Hardworking	Patient
Ambitious	Healthy	Patriotic
Athletic	Helpful	Pleasant
Brave	Honest	Positive
Classical	Humble	Reverent
Clean	Humorous	Revolutionary
Courteous	Hypnotic	Scholarly
Creative	Inventive	Thrifty
Dignified	Kind	Tithing
Forgiving	Loyal	Tranquil
Graceful	Manly	Well-dressed
Handsome	Meditative	Wide Awake
	Obedient	

I tentatively included Uncle Charlie's "What Works Works" but I couldn't make it an official virtue until I understood what he meant.

Every night for weeks before Mirabella exploded into the tower, I marked myself on virtues: a red crayon for flunking, a black crayon for passing. If I flunked I marked "minus one" or "minus ten" and vice versa for passing. If I flunked horribly enough I circled it in red. Each day some went untested and weren't marked.

At fourteen and one-half years old, I had three and one-half years until deadline. As I imagined it then I'd be in curly-crew with ear lobe sideburns, leftover pimples powdered, nose disguised, a serious expression capturing the *People* reader—hand on chin, wrinkled forehead, eyes darting from the photo in a steely now-see-here glance.

One of the toughest virtues to pass each night was Job's "Patient." The days seemed to ooze by. But I knew I'd get that cover by eighteen. It was as tight as mathematics.

The day of Hunnicut's attack was disastrous in another way—I ran into St. George. After she danced her blues at grandpop's funeral, St. George grew up into a girl, sort of. She was pudgy with an upside-down oriole nest hairdo intertwined with plastic prayer beads. She wrapped herself in a kind of sari of black-dyed burlap with her armpits showing because she was sprouting black hair there and wanted to show it off—a lot more hair because she had flunked and was sixteen. She thought she knew more too, through drugs and glue.

One day of each month she celebrated the birthday of Siva, the Hindu God of Death. She swooped around the halls in a black burlap cape with "Happy Birthday Siva" spelled in white cloth bones on the back. She said he was born over four hundred billion years ago. Every week she danced into the towers with a new Siva button pinned to her darn sari, her answer to Col. Cole's mottos.

"Siva Venit!" one said. She imagined this was proved by the wars and genocides of this century. She insisted there's never been so much Siva in the air; she expected the Second Coming any day now. Also, any day now, she pledged to show her devotion to Siva by committing suicide in front of the Memorial Tombstone. She had to make the momentous choice between burning at the peak or swan diving from the Tomb onto a plank of railroad spikes.

St. George imagined that all humans begin to die from the instant they are born. Death is certain, she said, and added that it's a sure thing that all humans try to do will be destroyed by time. Since all is doomed, effort is meaningless, she preached.

Col. Cole tried like crazy to help her; he even gave her free overtime sessions with the school shrink.

St. George said our lives are streams of trivialties. Only when we arrive at the moment of death did we realize the height of meaning.

The streams of trivialities should be replaced with rivers of depression, she said.

She acted out every day by practicing her depth dance in the halls.

At first none of the other kids put up with this hamming, but after a while they tolerated her, forgetting their morals, as usual. "Well, it's just toad squatting," they laughed and walked around her.

I didn't give up so easy. I yelled a fiery word or two at her. If she was being really dirty in her exercises, I booted her. I would have done worse, but I remembered the nice job she did at grandpop's funeral.

One day she went completely bats, bounding into school in topless black leotards, beating her chests and babbling that Siva's astrological signs were in direct conglomeration. She urged us all to commit suicide by depressing ourselves to death.

Col. Cole kept his cool and only whipped a three-day suspension on her. She never pulled that leotard stunt again.

While sitting in the boy's bathroom, I overheard a kid saying she did dirty things with mobs of guys, even Shop L lunatics. I decided then and there she was a mortal threat to everybody's morals and that night I rigged up a dummy out of one of mom's pillowcases, bunching a ball of yarn and beads for the hair and draping a dirty burlap sack around the pillow. To it I safety-pinned a sign "St. George, Foe of the American

Way." In the morning I dangled the dummy from F. D. R's flagpole on the roof.

Kids arriving on the buses got a giggle out of that.

St. George took it differently—she fell in love with me. Moaning that I was determined to destroy her, she said I was Siva's agent. She begged me to take her out on a date. She chased me all over school, sighing that I had beautiful murderer's eyes and that Siva was surely in contact with me. She wouldn't be surprised if someday I appeared in a black cape, revealed myself as Siva's undercover man, and slaughtered her.

After geography, the same day Hunnicut attacked, I climbed the ladder to the main floor, on my way to algebra. A girl's voice hollered for help. St. George lay flat on her back next to the girls' elevator, her legs in the air and her sari around her neck. A Grey Area told me she'd been showing off a new creation and had slipped during her final "Leap Into the Grave."

I hurried over and picked her up and carried her down to the school nurse while the kids catcalled behind me. See, I saved her on instinct without thinking who she was; I would have flunked Helpful and Kind if I didn't follow my instinct.

So I got a bit of Job's medicine. The school paper published a limerick about "a dancing toad

73

and her beanpole beau." The night of the rescue, the phone rang just as I was settling down to mark my chart. "Kip, your eyes were very murderous today. You've been in communication with Siva maybe?"

I slammed down the receiver and rushed to my dormer window alcove before anything else happened to lower the record for the day. Here's how it wound up.

NO ACTION

Obedient—Nobody ordered me so I didn't have a chance to obey.

Tithing—It wasn't Sunday.

Thrifty—By then I'd blown all my allowance and didn't have any to be thrifty with.

Forgiving—Nobody worth forgiving did anything to forgive.

What Works Works—I didn't understand.

PLUS

Pleasant—I marked plus two for saving St. George.

Reverent—Plus two because I forgot three prepositions in the English quiz. When I put through a prayer to God, the Holy Ghost slipped me the answers and I scored eighty-five. Also, when Hunnicut tried that trick, I almost took God's name in vain but stopped before it ever got to the thought stage.

Patriotic—After the fight with Hunnicut, I brainstormed the idea to battle the enemy when they invaded California, The Anti-Enemy League. We'd have a Hard Core of three hundred kids who'd give up anything for the League and do anything to stamp out the menace. The Hard Core would be top secret and only meet in underground shelters. We'd agree to inform on each other and kill our own mother if ordered. There'd be a secret password and handshake and everybody's home would be bugged. Outside the Hard Core there'd be a Semi-Core of 7,000 kids who believed in freedom but couldn't be trusted enough for Hard Core. Outside of that would be the Non-Core of Grey Areas who thought the right way but would be useful only for the final battle and paying dues. There might be a million of these. The radio tower in back of my house would be a good haranguing spot, like the Pope's balcony. I'd have to get cracking and hack out the woods around it.

That was worth plus thirty on Patriotic.

Loyal—I marked plus one for steadfastly admitting it was her I helped in the hall.

Honest—same mark, same reason.

Kind—I marked plus one for saving St. George.

Hardworking—plus three for thinking up the Anti-Enemy League.

The same for Ambitious, Revolutionary and Creative.

Athletic—plus five because I ran an extra mile in cross-country. Same for Healthy.

Meditative—Since it was taking more than ten minutes to fill out the chart, I marked plus one.

Handsome—I abstained from eating a Milky Way bar which gave me plus two for pimples.

Helpful—I discovered a piece of paper in the hall that a Grey Area dropped on purpose. I picked it up before old Mr. Benjamin, the janitor, had to bend down and probably throw his back out. I carried it to the hole and, after sending down a seventh grader to check for Hunnicut, I climbed down and found Mr. Benjamin standing in the shadows. I handed him the piece of paper.

Inventive—plus fifty. After St. George called I invented the idea of a button that would trigger a phony explosion and automatically disconnect the telephone, saving me the trouble of hanging up discourteously and maybe flunking virtues. This would also be handy with Mirabella when she returned.

Positive—plus fifty for approaching the unwanted phone calls positively.

MINUS

Hypnotic—minus fifty. I forgot to do the next lesson in *Hypnosis To Amaze Your Neighbors.*

Brave—minus thirty for the Hunnicut fight. I was easy with myself because I wasn't sure if it really happened, all that drilling and yelling and singing. I marked off another seventy here for the St. George disaster. Total in Brave was minus one hundred.

Loyal—since I was disloyal to all I stood for with St. George, I marked minus one hundred. With the plus one for admitting it, the score came out minus ninety-nine.

Tranquil—same as Loyal and Brave for both Hunnicut and St. George, minus two hundred.

Wide Awake—minus one hundred for saving her without thinking.

Honest—I acted like I cared about her when actually I disapproved of her and ought to have let her know it for her own good. Minus one hundred, which, with the plus one for admitting it, came out to minus ninety-nine.

Humorous—minus fifty for the joke that failed with Sharon Singer. While she waited for the temporary elevator, I pushed the darn call button for her and bowed low like a Louis XIV courtier. She turned her back. I flunked

Graceful, Manly, Dignified and Classical with the same mark for the same reason.

Approaching the end of the virtues, I considered Courteous, Well-dressed and Clean.

I shuddered when I remembered St. George squatting on the other end of the line in her hairy sari. A strange accident happened to me. I wished I was born without hands, or had the luck of Harry Jenks who was working on a war helicopter project in shop and raised his hand to ask a question and had it lopped off by the blade.

I sinned because the state forced me to rub elbows with swarthy Peter Hunnicut from Shop L. Some kids said he was an Arab. Shop L was the class for dummies who scored below eighty-five I.Q. and Hunnicut was enrolled there each year except seventh, when he made a miraculous ninety-five.

They tried to teach these dopes how to snip wastebaskets out of ice cream containers and how to blow their noses without a mess and how to kick a ball and even catch it. The main thing was they tried to teach them the rules of civilization so they wouldn't bother anybody. They didn't get into higher laws, because that would be hopeless, like teaching a reptile to say "please," I figured.

There were twenty-one in Shop L, nineteen guys and two girls. They called it Shop L because it met in the boiler room behind the shop and I guess that L stood for lunatic. It wasn't a half-bad boiler room, with used desks, a black-board and travel posters of Spain. The lunatics couldn't complain, after all it was free. The state forced taxpayers to support the program, which wasn't right, I thought. Why should my mom and pop have to chip in for other people's sins?

Sin made the kids stupid, either their per-sonal sins, or the parents' sin or their grandpar-ents', like the Bible says. Hunnicut's family was crammed with sin. His swarthy father was out-standing down at City Hall, strapped on a wooden plank with roller skate wheels, tooting a harmonica. He was born without legs because of a sex disease. Hunnicut's mom lost her legs in a twenty-four hour laundry, where she still worked, propped on a stool folding underwear.

Hunnicut was paying dues for his own sins too, like Pride. He was stuck up because he was the only other guy with much hair around his pri-vates: I had some, he had some. But I kept my undershorts on under my gym outfit so I wouldn't make a big scene when I undressed in the locker room. I wasn't about to be an exhibitionist.

Hunnicut paraded around naked and once for a joke he tangled a daisy in his kinky hair. The boys got such a giggle out of it that they ballyhooed him for President of the Student Senate.

In all past years the normal students didn't have to be polluted by Shop L kids. Then this year the state gave in to some anarchist agitators and ruled that lunatics had to join in our classes. Some left-wing professor dreamed up a theory that they'd catch good principles. He forgot that we might catch bad stuff from them. In the first integrated homeroom, Hunnicut squirted a fountain pen on his pants. Mr. Hines, who knew that sin was communicable, ordered him to sit in the hall for the rest of the year. Col. Cole kept Hunnicut right in line, whistling whenever he saw him. Even if he wasn't doing anything at all wrong, he tweeted him down to remind him who was boss.

What Col. Cole really hated was Hunnicut's bushy mustache. According to state law he couldn't make him shave it off because Hunnicut was a member of a minority group. Like I said, most figured he was an Arab. But Hunnicut didn't play fair: for an after-school job he insisted he was a majority Italian; when it came to his mustache, he turned Arab overnight.

The state forced me to associate with Hunnicut and I held it responsible for infecting me. All of a sudden it was growing bigger and bigger, feeling like nothing I'd ever felt before. I heard footsteps on the stair carpet but I didn't care. Then it felt the best and made a mess. I pulled the meditation alcove curtain and bowed my head. Through the sheet pop saw my silhouette.

He respects my prayers and he shut the door and went back downstairs.

I ran into the bathroom and cleaned up. Using mom's cuticle scissors I beheaded the hairs one by one and collected their heads in my palm and flushed them down and away. I only wished I was brave enough to yank out the roots.

While I lay awake trying to sleep, I thought up a new virtue and coded it "Clean Towels," a disguise in case biographers unearthed the chart while examining my Library of Congress papers. I marked Clean Towels a minus five hundred for the first night, making it the most miserable day for virtue I'd ever had.

I meditated about that for the rest of the night, while Willy whined for me to come to bed. I told him to shut up; what did half-breed coyotes know about sin? "Please God, never let me doubt You or Your virtue again. Forgive all my sins and please don't punish me too bad. Thomas doubted and yet You made him a saint. In Jesus' name. Amen."

Right away H. G.'s Invisible Hand latched on to my throat and strangled me until I was half dead. I knew the reason He let Hunnicut infect me—He was guiding me like always, warning me to steer clear of Hunnicut, because he was the mortal enemy of the Ultimate Heir.

The next morning I found a dollar lying on the tile under the toilet. I carried it to the kitchen and asked mom if it was hers. She said no, and pop said the same thing.

It was a sign. I shouldn't worry too much about flunking Clean Towels: His Hand fixed that sin. This was cash for church, so I'd pass Tithing that week. H. G. gave me the dollar to give back.

Nine

THERE were no announcements this year about how we were supposed to be nice to Mirabella. Mr. Hines just said she'd received evolutionary treatment over the summer and was expected to return momentarily. A few wise guys turned and grinned at me while I sat hunched over at my desk, trying to imagine myself frowning from *People.*

The late whistle sounded and Mirabella hadn't showed up. I prayed that this time she'd really dropped dead in the halls. The homeroom sergeant-at-arms, left his desk and spot checked us in the motto for the week. He was halfway through the Pledge of Allegiance when Col. Cole blasted his whistle outside our door. This wasn't unusual, but the shrieking after it was. We listened for Col. Cole's retaliating bellow to rattle the chalk trays. But he'd gone strangely quiet.

The door slammed open in a spray of glass. This vision raced into the room! The vision darted its head around and plopped itself in a front row seat, sobbing until its blond hair dripped tears from the ends.

Mr. Hines bent over and tried to comfort the vision, his crop of neck hives bulging more than usual. But Mirabella didn't give up. She hammered her desk and screamed. Mr. Hines took a broom from the closet and began sweeping up the glass. The whistle for the first class sounded but nobody moved or blinked.

We weren't staring because she yelled at Col. Cole or broke the door or threw the tantrum, but because she was no longer stained by sin! Her golden hair shimmered like the summer sun off the Cape May harbor; her face, even soggy with tears, was a "model of Nordic perfection," as Mr. Hines whispered; her bottomless blue eyes, her robin's egg blue t-shirt clinging to large round chests, her long naked legs stomping the floor under the desk. . . .

We stared, and Mirabella cursed Col. Cole for the rest of the period. Mr. Hines pretended to be too busy with the glass to remind us to move.

In a few days, the story of her cure spread through the halls.

While I was eating alone at the eighth grade buffet, Mirabella had been gasping in an oxygen tent, receiving the last Mohican rites from Reverend Hocheisen. A nurse gave her a clipping from *Stand Up For Evolution Journal.* Brushing the scales from her eyes, she read about Dr. Ebenezer's butte top clinic, but she was so far gone she let the clipping drop out of the tent. Her father found it on the floor five minutes later. Inside of another five minutes she was stowed in the back of his Lear jet on her way to the New Mexico desert.

Dr. Ebenezer was famous all over the West for his theory of psychoanalysis, "Remnants In Progress." According to Dr. Ebenezer, homo sapien Americans have been on a super-fast evolutionary escalator since the year 1776. His popular motto, filched off *Reader's Digest,* was "Every day in every way we're getting better and better."

The Remnant half of his theory was that some mentally messed up Americans dropped off the escalator and reverted to past stages of evolution. In really bad cases, because of a huge disappointment in love or business, they returned to viruses, molds and funguses. These people were beyond his help and he admitted it, turning them over to medical specialists.

But others reverted a shorter distance to a more recent remnant. Dr. Ebenezer treated such cases in his laboratories on the summit of a tall desert butte.

When her father's jet landed, the butte was smothered with patients waiting for treatment. Sunning themselves in lawn chairs were leather-skinned turtle people. Relaxing under the rocks in the rock garden were those past help, the viruses, molds and funguses. They actually had been thrown out of the clinic but stayed on, hiding and hoping against hope. Dr. Ebenezer, who had a heart of gold, looked the other way.

Since Mirabella was practically a goner and her dad was able to persuade Dr. Ebenezer with lots of cash, Mirabella's treatment began immediately. Dr. Ebenezer himself held all-day sessions with her, trying to figure out why she'd picked the remnant of the fish. The sessions seemed to keep her alive on hope. Finally, after a month of talks, when Dr. Ebenezer had just about lost his cool, Mirabella told him about the time in the root trap. She remembered the little minnows flitting about in the polluted stream and how she longed to be as free as they were.

Without another word, Dr. Ebenezer strapped her into a diver's helmet and dropped her into an aquarium filled with primitive coelacanths. He confined her underwater for five days, every thirty seconds shocking the heck out of her. The shocks killed the fish and they were left floating around and more coelacanths were dumped in. At the end of the five days, Mirabella was buried in smelly coelacanths and in a semi-coma from the electric shocks. But all her scales had peeled off; she wasn't ever again bothered by gills or webbed feet.

After this success, Dr. Ebenezer demanded an extra fifty thousand. But Mirabella and her pop skipped town to Idaho. There a doctor in Pocatello prescribed a mouthwash for her breath and a special underarm, foot and body deodorant exactly measured for her sweat glands. In Boise, she consulted a scalp specialist who regenerated her hair with an elixir distilled from the rare dew of an Idaho January. As an extra free of charge gift, because he admired the work of Dr. Ebenezer, he colored her eyes in a shade he dubbed "Limitless Blue."

From Boise she jetted to North Dakota and the General Dynamics building. In the company caves under the building, her Mako teeth were yanked and replaced with human teeth left over from the war. The doctors left out her back molars to make her cheeks sink in fashionably. They removed her chin and replaced it with a plastic one just firm enough for the rest of her face. Showing her Marilyn Monroe flicks, they taught her to let her chin hang down just a bit, leaving her mouth slightly open. In the drastic surgery cave they rebuilt the inside of her respiratory system to stop obnoxious fish noises and they grafted somebody's skin over what was left of her gill slits. Finally they chopped eleven inches off her ankles and readjusted her frame.

At a hospital in Utah she was injected with mastodon fossil extracts in her chests and hips. She exercised for a month in an out-patient clinic to develop support muscles for her new assets.

At the end of the summer, in an Oregon mountain clinic, she was primed with female chimpanzee hormones to make her feel like a full-time woman. They also transplanted the chimp's sex organs. "Now you're ten years *ahead* of the rest of our species," the doctor said, patting her bottom.

On the way back, her father touched down in New York and blew $10,000 on clothes and make-up. The beauticians plucked out her eyebrows and painted on new ones in the latest mode; they pried out her finger and toe nails and glued on stylish fiberglass replacements; they permanently removed the catfish hairs from her upper lip and the rest of her. For an extra fee, they banished the wax from her ears for good. She latched on to a year's supply of dresses, lingerie, t-shirts, shoes and wigs.

On the day I was meaninglessly attacked by Hunnicut, she roared back into International Airport.

Within a week Mirabella was elected treasurer of the homeroom, a member of the Student Senate, the Girls' Honor Committee and the American Committee to Bandage Lepers. In one month, she was Head of the Baking Committee for the Football Fund, Senate Nominating Committee Chairman, Vice President of the school and she was voted most popular and most likely to succeed by the school paper.

The Unitarians named her "Miss Open Mind" and sat her in her own convertible during the Thanksgiving Day Parade. The Ethical Culture Society proclaimed her "the student with the best all-around attitude to things."

Everybody agreed that Mirabella was the unofficial president and secretary and everything else of the in-crowd.

I thanked God that she was free from the brand of her unknown sin. She had been cleansed through H. G.'s workings. Some people said it was just plain Science. But I imagined it was more of a Miracle of Forgiveness.

I also figured she owed me a payment for saving her life and for being her escort when she was disgustingly sick. She'd have to pick me for her boy friend.

Ten

IN study hall I addressed the envelope "Airmail, General Delivery, care of Horace, King of Fireflies, Cadenza Castle Mail Room."

"Dear Grandpop,

"I'm writing because I'm in love for the first time. Listen, I need that specification. Do you think you could send the words by return mail, special delivery? You know, the magic flyspec.

"In the meantime I think I'll make out o.k. I've thought up this Virtue Chart and this morning four pimples were heading with pus and six were almost dried up. I've got other rewards too, like from this fellow Col. Cole, my principal. He's one of my favorite people down here.

"The main thing I admire about him is he tries to get kids to think; not that he's any profound prophet, like you, but he does try. Every week he makes the school learn a new motto and sometimes really shakes up their processes. And if the motto doesn't do it, the whistle does.

"That's the whistle he got in the Pacific. In assemblies he liked to tell us how the general had him down in the bamboo, glaring at him with doped up eyes. But Col. Cole never quit for a second. He yanked a knife out of the gook's own boot and stabbed him in the ear. He lifted the gold whistle but of course left him the pictures of his wife and children.

"I was just stuffing my books in my geography desk, when Col. Cole hustled through the halls tweeting the signal for Special Assembly. I rode the elevator kind of nervous to the top of the eighth grade tower. In assembly hall, I sat under the glass roof, staring at the windy sky, feeling the tower rocking back and forth beneath me. From the distance, I heard his tweeter giving out detentions to slowpokes and daydreamers. As the two hundred piece boys' band struck up 'Cheers to the Chief,' we stood at attention. He ran down the aisle blasting above the music and darting his finger at hackers in the audience. He threw out Hunnicut on general principles. Hunnicut's one of the lowest . . . but I won't get into that since this has to be light enough for airmail.

"Col. Cole ordered Mass Exercise to begin and teachers and kids jogged in place in time to his blasts—Col. Cole's preparation for Oriental Invasion. He yelled out names—Larry's, Sharon's and mine—and we trotted to the stage in time to his whistle while five thousand pairs of bouncing eyes concentrated on us. Wow, was I shook! I didn't know what was coming up; maybe we'd done something horrible that I didn't know was supposed to be horrible yet!

"Col. Cole bounded down the aisle and handsprang onto the stage. He waved his lanyard overhead and led the school in a Long Yell Excelsior, his favorite cheer. See, he doesn't allow girl cheerleaders because kids look up their dresses. I was so close to him I was afraid he'd land on me coming down off a jump. "Valley Forge Joint! Valley Forge Joint! We Beat Valley Forge Joint! Excelsior!" he hollered, leaping high on the last bit with his school tie in his face and his whistle flapping and his pants cuffs hiking above his knees to his school color garters. He landed with a three hundred pound bang and whirled his arms like a double windmill and pirouetted on one toe and took off again screaming 'Excelsior!'

"He told the parents present that he was cheering because we had beaten Valley Forge Joint in the annual Cosmetic and Shoe Derby. Our boys sold $9,000 worth of shoes at $10.98 a pair, door to door, and our girls did over $3,000 in lipstick and mascara. Not bad, huh? That meant we got a matching gift from the Ford Foundation and all the cash went to Col. Cole's Memorial Tombstone in front of the ninth grade tower. Grads were buried there no matter what war they died in.

"Col. Cole had his face on the cover of *People* last year, sitting on Ike's stuffed camel. He'd been flipping through some old school records when he came across the name of a kid buried in Arlington National Cemetery, a First World War vet. He phoned the Pentagon and demanded we get the kid for the Tombstone. They hung up on him. He fought all the way to the Supreme Court and got his photo. I was an official usher the day they buried the remains wrapped in our school flag. I wish you'd been there to see me, grandpop.

"The funds this year went to a matching pair of North Vietnamese machine guns that screwed on top of two World War Two Nazi midget subs that rode the backs of two armor-plated stuffed camels from Ike's invasion of Lebanon. They're always tearing down and building up the towers, but Col. Cole won't let the school board touch the Tombstone. People forget too easy the boys who have died for them, he says. For another practical thing, the 25¢ tomb admission fee goes to Milk for War Orphans. That is a charity he founded.

"Col. Cole called the motto bearers to the stage and asked the audience to get out pencils and copy down 'The harder you polish the pearl, the more it gleams.' I pretended to write but my hand was shaking too much. My breakfast rose in my throat but I forced it back down, using my tongue as a stopper. Col. Cole asked mom and pop to take a bow and pop waved at me. 'Kipper, my boy,' Col. Cole breathed into the microphone, 'stand up and come on over here.'

"He laid his hands up on my shoulders and spoke warm words about my perseverance, about how I hadn't let rainy weather keep me inside, etc. He listed ten of the virtues on the Chart, which shows you I must be onto something at least.

"It turns out my $687.58 worth of shoes was good for second place. He dragged out the eighty-eight link Silver Second Place Chain and wrapped it around my head with the end dangling down behind. The darn thing hurt. 'We hereby crown a lad whose character has provided our students with a symbol of healthy manliness,' Col. Cole proclaimed, slapping my back. The band struck up 'The Thunderer' while the audience stood in tribute.

"So you see, grandpop, I'm getting by. Mirabella was in the audience—that's the girl I love. I'm sure I saw her clapping longer than the others. I waved to her but she didn't wave back. She's a wonderful person, with a nice figure and is very popular with kids and teachers. But I can see it might be tough. Even though I saved her from a trap when she was little, virtue may not be enough in this case. I know it's a sin to think that and I hope H. G. will forgive me, but I'm crazy with love. So how about the magic words?!!

"Another thing I wanted to ask you, how come you didn't reply to my letter? I sent you one last year with a return address but I never heard anything about it. Did you get it? I enclosed a clipping about archeologists finding curious slabs in Australia decorated with primitive drawings of fireflies. There were freaky inscriptions on it, four or five words that nobody could make out. Some scientist tried to pronounce them and immediately took off into the air! I didn't know if that info would be interesting to you or not. Anyway, would you please, please, please write back so I get a fighting chance with Mirabella? The rewards for virtue are slow, some days.

"And anything I can do for you, let me know.

I still shine the bike and change the batteries once a month.

"Please send those words like you promised.

Love, Kip"

Eleven

AFTER cross-country practice, I was sauntering past the eighth grade tower on my way to the student parking lot, books slung over my shoulder, my head weighed down with my eighty-eight links. I inched my head back to enjoy the cool breeze whistling through my crown.

At the top of the tower what seemed to be a butterfly was flapping around Abe's statue. But this butterfly had a purpose in mind, so maybe it was a bird, I thought. Then it drifted from the shadows behind Abe's chair and became a piece of paper folded like an airplane. Some trashy Grey Area had thrown it from a window and it would glide gradually to earth and probably clutter up the grounds about midnight.

I was almost to my car when I remembered: since St. George had tried to take a flyer from the twenty-fifth floor, all the windows up that high were nailed shut. At that instant the plane smacked me a square shot on the nose. It lay on its back, one wing fluttering as if injured. The seal of the Governor was printed on the tip of the injured wing. Under the seal it said "Important Notice!"

This notice had been posted in Col. Cole's announcement box and I'd done nothing about it. Reminding myself to flunk "Wide Awake," I bent down to pick it up.

It was folded like no paper plane I'd ever dug, sort of a modified Delta wing with a gold paper clip on its re-entry nose cone.

"Big Opportunity for Junior Scholars!" it read. "Enter Teen Scholar Contest! First Prize, a four year full-tuition college scholarship and luncheon with the Governor of Your State. Second Prize, a two year full-tuition college scholarship. Third Prize, a weekend retreat with author Danielle Steel. Plus hundreds of honorable mention certificates!

There were five categories to enter: "The Workings of Volcanoes; An Experiment in Psychology; The Oceans as Farms; An Original Fiction Composition; Anti-Matter and Anti-World."

It said to enter your proposed category no later than midnight of that day. They'd review it and send approval to proceed.

I hopped in the car and drove figure-eights around the parking lot, revving up my I.Q.

I thought about St. George's Messenger of Depression, a ten foot tall black metal angel sporting a thirty foot wing-span. In homeroom science fair, when she switched it on for the judges, it flapped itself to death, chucking parts of its body all over the room and conking a judge. They were sorry for her until she told them it was supposed to do that.

I decided on my entry.

I whipped off a letter and mailed it, registered, special delivery.

While driving home, I wondered some more about that paper plane.

Twelve

WEEKS passed and I didn't hear a word from Washington. Mirabella took up with Hunnicut.

There *were* explanations why a swell girl like Mirabella would have an affair with the Missing Link. For instance, she might have been impressed because he was a football jock: he couldn't catch or remember plays, but if the quarterback pointed him in the right direction he ran like a rhino.

I figured the real truth went deeper. She still had a hankering for lower evolutionary types. She'd made it through the guppies, but Hunnicut, with his primitive hang-up on hair, filled the bill for now. Sin scored the first touchdown.

Football season would end in a few days. Mirabella would lose her infatuation with the prehistoric. She'd re-dig me and ditch him.

Of course, after I snagged the Second Place Chain, I had my choice. There was Sharon Singer, Larry's girl, with the kind of chests you don't even see on the tube. Because of her chests, she was almost as popular as Mirabella. One plus she had on Mirabella was the rumor she had an abortion in the summer. Right after this zipped around, the in-kids worshipped her because she seemed avant garde. Sharon didn't deny the awful gossip, explaining it was Hunnicut's fetus and they had to do it because she aimed for junior college and Hunnicut had his heart set on owning a gas station. Also, Hunnicut was a Baptist and Sharon was a Semite. Their parents jumped into it over the religion issue and set up the operation in a hospital upstate near Scranton.

I could have forgiven the abortion, since forgiveness was on the Chart and Sharon was certainly *worth* forgiving, but the major drawback with Sharon was her records. In academic reports she didn't do so hot in Latin and History and she had twelve days suspension on her conduct report. Her athletic record was just as rotten, no goals in hockey and no sit-ups in gymnastics. If she was going to be any help to me I'd have to ask her to do something about that, but it seemed like too much bother.

Anyway I examined it, Mirabella was the one. A romance between us would make me top dog in the whole school and give me a flying start to *People.*

Besides her popularity, Mirabella would be politically helpful. After *People,* I'd be running for some kind of state or national office and her command of the History of the Western World course would be handy. I didn't look over her shoulder once and see a history grade less than ninety-five. She racked up a hundred on the V.P.'s of the U.S. surprise quiz when everybody else, except me, flunked. Mirabella remembered all the V.P.'s and just for kicks threw in all fifty states and their governors.

She'd be super in managing the family financial affairs. As homeroom treasurer she never once came out in the red, even when other homerooms lost their shirts in the party for war orphans. One of the orphans blasted open the school safe and took off with $750.48. Col. Cole told the kids they'd have to pay back the funds or stay in session weekends running a car wash. Our homeroom was the only one that made its quota.

I had some worries about Mirabella's Bohemian Godlessness. But I figured she'd had a good church upbringing and should be easy to re-convert.

The night after the last football game, I skipped my homework, grunted through a few pushups and sat down in the meditation alcove to plot the script. I wrote out seven drafts with loads of fail-safe features. I swallowed a few of mom's sleeping pills and hit the sack.

Unfortunately, I overslept and the zing wasn't there: I didn't have any of that finger popping business that I have when I'm in fine shape.

The next problem was getting to Mirabella before Hunnicut met her and escorted her to the elevator for the first class. As an officer of the homeroom, Mirabella would lead opening exercises and exit three minutes early for her warden post, right down the hall. Hunnicut's boiler room was in the basement. There was no reason why I couldn't get to her with a whole floor on him.

I wasn't about to take any chances though. I stacked my books, put a hand on my knee and got set. Mirabella fastened up her warden straps and out she went, a little late at 8:44.

On the whistle, I charged, hitting the door before the other kids were even out of their seats. It banged open too hard, but at least I was in the hall before the herd. The script was clicking. But by flunking Wide Awake again, I didn't see the door bouncing back; the knob wanged into the pile of books in my left hand and they skittered here and there around the darn hall. The worst of it was that the outline for our English autobiography was due that day and all ten pages flew into the air.

By a miracle I managed to catch up with them and not one had a shoe mark on it. That left me two and a half minutes before the late whistle. Of course, by the time the stampede had cleared and I was ready to go, Hunnicut had outraced me and they were far down the hall, waltzing along to geography. She didn't seem a bit interested in getting to her post.

As dignified as possible, I half walked and half ran up behind them. Gracefully, I tapped Mirabella on the shoulder. I thought she'd look around and see it was me, her old hero, and maybe stop and let Hunnicut go on by himself. But like a dope I tapped the wrong shoulder and she turned the wrong way. "No hands in the hall, Petie," she giggled. The Arab barbarian smiled at her like she was playing a cute game. He didn't spot me, thank goodness. I tapped her left shoulder.

"Hiya," I said, courteously, humbly and pleasantly.

"What do *you* want?"

"A word with you in private, please."

"What?" she said, impolitely.

"Just a sec. It's important," I said, patiently, with kindness.

She shrugged her shoulders and looked at Hunnicut and Hunnicut scowled at me while I led her over to a metal water fountain. "Mirabella ah . . . I've been wanting to ask you something for a long time. I think we should take up again where we left off in dancing class. Would you like to go to the movies?" I said, forgetting all my lines at once.

That big jock rushed over and wacked me a knuckle punch in the left bicep. "Piss off pus puss," he growled. Mirabella got hysterical. I guess she thought he was very witty for making up an alliteration: she was studying that for English extra credit.

I opted not to face him down for the moment, since Mirabella was laughing so insanely it would have been impossible to communicate. I scooped up my autobiography before Hunnicut got a look at it, and I retreated, stopping as soon as I turned the corner of the hall. I unloaded my books and rubbed my arm and tried to get my mind to think.

After thirty seconds of rubbing, I peeked one eye out and saw them holding hands, mushing along at the end. I dodged down the hall, winging silently on my toes until I got positioned behind her on my face's good side. "Mirabella, did you know my Uncle Charlie just bought me a Corvette for my birthday?"

I saw this info register in her eyes. Hunnicut snuck one foot behind me and shoved me over. When I woke up, the late whistle was tweeting and my nose was a mess.

I staggered to the infirmary and told the nurse I'd fallen down hustling to class. She wrote out a leave of absence which was lucky because the autobiography was blood-soaked and would have to be typed over. It was miraculous that Hunnicut knocked me cold, otherwise I'd have flicked a few karate shots at him and put his lights out.

All sorts of mysteries reared up: like who permitted Mirabella to fall in love with the Mongoloid? For sure her dad didn't. Mirabella came from a solid home; her family was one of the richest. Heck, Mirabella's mom was a Sunday School teacher in the Neighborhood Church. Well then, who permitted it?

It was very irrational. I considered the cave man thoroughly as I lay with ice on my face, my nose stuffed with cotton and my head dropped over the side of the bed. It wasn't only that he was stupid and proud and put daisies in his private hair; he also had rotten manners, like what he said about my complexion when I was doing everything, bending over backwards to make it clear up.

It was depressing as cancer. All fall the kids had gone crazy for him in the stands, screaming murder at the coach whenever he benched Hunnicut and making up ridiculous chants about his heroic name. Now he was going out for basketball.

And he had won Mirabella! But I had saved her life!

I eased up my head. I didn't discover any blood when I tugged out the cotton so I chucked it and sat down in the alcove to mark the chart for the day: minus one thousand for Dignified, circling the score in red; I marked plus one for Aggressive since I *did* try twice.

Blood splattered on the chart. I pushed it away. My skull was beginning to ache something horrendous.

Thirteen

I pulled on my red and white school color pajamas and slipped into what used to be the family bowling alley. All the walls and the ceiling were white now. There was a white dresser with a glass of vitamin fortified milk and a white plate of vanilla cookies. Whenever Kathy woke up she sipped the milk and nibbled the cookies and bowled duckpins if she felt like it. We knew she had waked up because the milk and cookies were gone. On her good days, we heard the rumble of her ball.

At night a small porcelain clown holding a dim light bulb kept Kathy company. In the day the sun shined through the white draperies and her room gleamed like heaven. The queen-sized bed with rubber sheets and high sides was the only other furniture.

I moved over the cat and climbed in with Kathy, reaching for her hand under the covers. She stirred and gave her hand to me, but didn't wake up.

I lay back in daydreams, watching the room from far in the universe. An alarm clock went off. Kathy sat up, smiling and stretching, and switched off the alarm. When she hopped out of bed, I saw she was much more developed than usual. Her white-blond hair hung to her round bottom. She pulled back the drapes and sunlight swooped into the dust cloud. Wearing an Atlantic City Bowling Team t-shirt with deep V neck, she did her feminine wake-up exercises, wrist-thrusts, toe-touches, the upside-down bicycle. With her emerald studded Duncan, she yo-yoed Around The World and Over the Falls.

The door eased open and I entered in slow motion.

Later we yanked off the white sheets and bowled, Kathy leaning low to the alley, her chests cradling the ball. She scored 260, 285 and 300, which beat me hands down.

There was a muffled noise. I snapped up in complete darkness. I heard it again outside the door. "Kipper," pop whispered, "come on now. Don't you know I hate that?" He must have heard the darn springs.

I let go Kathy's hand. She felt around for it, then went quiet.

Back in my room, I lay next to Willy and tried to sleep, but my mind was jangling like a burglar alarm. Going in there meant I'd flunk Classical, Obedient, Positive, Patient and an accidental C. T. But I liked Kathy; I loved her. I didn't feel even a little bit guilty.

In the alcove I ran through the Chart, marking plus two for Creative, since I thought up the brainstorm of tempting Mirabella with my Corvette. Then I remembered that was a sin, bragging. I marked minus two for Humble.

I banged my hand down. They'd cancelled each other out! That was mystery enough. While I circled the scores, wisdom began seeping into my brain.

Virtue was a hoax!

For days the Chart had been near perfection, even C. T. But where did it get me? A bruised bicep, a bloody nose and further away than ever from *People*. At this rate assassination was the only way I'd make it, and I didn't even own a gun. Besides the way they protected the Presidents, I'd never even get near enough to buzzer his hand.

Sure, virtues seemed to have won me the

Chain, but maybe I'd have made it anyway. The same went for the paper plane reward. Sure, all the windows were nailed shut, but maybe a freak wind blew it up there. It was just one in a million that it hit my nose, just coincidence.

Since then pimples had launched a huge offensive against my nose, fifteen on the tip! Even on my ears! Virtue might have been handy against Job's boils but with pimples it's a dead duck. I tried harder than any kid I knew, but God had cut me off worse than the guy who forgot to tithe.

I grabbed the top corners of the Chart and ripped it down the middle, scoring in my last virtue, Tranquil, because I ripped it quietly and calmly, the long way, into bookmarks exactly half an inch wide. I opened the Government Printing Office's pamphlet, *Hypnosis to Amaze Your Neighbors.*

The floor creaked, followed by sniffing under the door. It was pop, double-checking about me and Kathy. I had time to bow my head. "To heck with that!" I thought, stubbing out the Lucky I'd just lit up.

The door opened and, when he saw what I was doing, slammed behind him. Pop couldn't believe it. He stood watching me for five minutes, still not sure if he smelled smoke. "Kipper, you know the rules about study hours," he complained finally, forgetting the Lucky.

"Yes, pop."

"Are you purposely doing this?"

"It's a Personal Growth Pamphlet from Washington, D.C."

"I don't give a darn where it's from. Now get busy with your Sunday School lesson or your homework."

He opened the Sunday School book and tried to jam a pencil between my fingers. I let it drop and kept on reading.

"Here! Here! What page are you at?"

"I forget. Besides grandpop said Sunday School's for naysayers."

"Now don't give me any of that stuff!" he said, trying to snatch the pamphlet. He circled the room and rushed back. "Look here, Kipper! This is necessary!" he said, thumping the book. I read a page and a half about hypnosis.

"Either that pamphlet goes or . . . " he threatened.

"Pop, hypnosis saves lives."

"Jesus is the only one that saves anything! You gave your life to Him! Get rid of that pamphlet!"

"Will you leave my room please, pop?"

"No!" he shouted, raising his hand, his eyes bulging with fear.

I heaved the Sunday School book at him. That shook him out of it. "I give my life to save him from the secular devil! Now he fouls his sister and *embraces* the secular devil! Win at the spigot and lose at the bung hole."

He sort of knelt, asking me to pray for forgiveness, bowing his head, reaching up for my hand, groping. "Honor thy father and thy mother that you may have a long life and prosperity in the land which the Lord your. . . . "

"Go to heck!" I said. Grabbing the pamphlet, I split.

Uncle Charlie gave me the Sting Ray for my fourteenth birthday. He handed the key to pop saying I could drive only if pop was with me and I got my learner's permit. I had another key made.

Uncle Charlie had baked a red "14" racing number into each door. I pasted two big red "M's" on the hood and the spoiler. My bomb sported genuine leather bucket seats, a stereo cassette player, Blaupunkt AM-FM-Short Wave, four horns honking four different tunes, a racing tac, rally clock, compass, power steering, four wheel power disc brakes, Le Mans seat harnesses, a roll bar and a four hundred horsepower, Turbo-Fire fuel injection racing triple two barrel that did one hundred seventy cruising.

I burned rubber up the road, blowing my chimes.

An hour later I hooked a right at the Atlantic Ocean.

I tooled past our Cape May summer house, all dark and boarded up. Shingles were blowing off. Sand drifted over the front walk. A family of stray cats was living under the porch. I tried the doors and shutters, but they were locked fast.

Through a crack in a shutter, I saw grand-pop's wicker rocker piled upside down in the living room. The t.v. faced the wall, disguised by yellowed newspapers and a vase of dried-up flowers.

I hiked through the dunes to the beach. Under the board-walk, peeking from the sand, I found grandpop's kayak. The canvas was blasted away by the sea winds. Only the wooden frame, some gear and the mast were left.

I dug them out and dragged the remains to the ocean side. After skewering the mast into the sand, I built up a wet sand bow and wet sand sides around the frame. Hunkering inside, I peered over the rough surf, waiting for the incoming tide.

I thought very hard about grandpop's magic words. But the harder I thought, the further they escaped into the past.

The summer that grandpop took his last sail was the summer they packed him off to the Golden Age. At the dinner table every night he had bellowed his poetry and bragged about his musical inventions.

Mom and pop wouldn't say a word in reply and they wouldn't let me speak to him either. I was only nine then. After dinner, grandpop rocked on the front porch, waving his cigar and talking to the clouds. If I tried to get near him, mom said, "That's enough now, Kipper."

Sometimes that summer he disappeared for days, visiting taverns and looking for people to talk to. He'd stumble back dirty and smelly and would be quiet as he lay in bed and tried to fix his head. As soon as he felt o.k. he wanted to talk again.

Late in the summer, mom announced they were going to commit him to the Golden Age. They got a court order and sold the house he had lived in with grandmom. They used the money to rent him a room in the G. A. Mom tried to make it sound like a lot of fun and games, but she didn't fool grandpop.

He began to lose control of his functions. At night he couldn't sleep through a few hours without making a mess. I'd wake up and hear his hands sliding along the walls, searching for the bathroom door. He never made it.

He cursed when he discovered what he'd done, "blast!" and woke up the whole house, stomping around and smashing his fists through the plaster and sometimes breaking mirrors and vases. Pop reminded him the more he sinned the sicker he'd get.

As the summer went on, grandpop got angrier and angrier at his body for not doing what it was supposed to do. Nobody was getting any sleep. Mom and pop couldn't wait for the day they would truck him away.

The day before the Golden Age people came for him, grandpop sat in his rocker with his hands hanging down behind him, staring out the window at the ocean. It was rough that day because we were into hurricane season and this storm was the tail end of one.

I sat looking out the window with him. Grandpop didn't try to talk to me and I didn't know what to say anyway.

At dinner, he wouldn't eat. He sat with his back turned, watching the blowing reeds on a dune.

When mom asked if she could cook him something special for his last night at home, grandpop didn't answer. She had just put on the Jello and whipped cream. Grandpop stomped upstairs to his room.

We ate Jello and listened to him banging around. Pop spread out the Bible and prepared to read the daily lesson. When grandpop started booming down the stairs, pop closed the Bible and hurried to block the front door.

Grandpop had on his hiking boots and his Irish hunting cape that was way too big for him and his black pointed Halloween hat. His flute was sticking out of his vest pocket.

Pop warned: "Sin leads to death. . . . " Grandpop smacked him one and pop fell whirling across the room onto the sofa while grandpop mashed the door behind him.

Mom phoned the police and Coast Guard. We waited in the living room until past midnight and they didn't snag him. Pop fell asleep in his chair. I lay down under some pillows on the sofa. Mom put an Afghan over me and the pillows and swaddled Kathy in her crib upstairs.

At two o'clock there was a whopping at the door. Pop jumped out of his chair and disappeared up the stairs. Fastening the chain, mom opened the door a crack. "You can't come in like that. Sleep it off on the porch."

"Be a human being."

"Well you can't bring her in here."

Grandpop bashed the glass out of the door and unlatched the chain. Mom ran out the back door. I pretended to be reading a comic.

Grandpop reached down and patted my head. "Kip, I want you to meet a fine lady." I stood up and shook hands with her. "She and me are engaged."

"That's nice," I said.

We all sat down.

She was the fat lady who ran the combination gasoline and flower place along the way to the shore. There was a rusty gas pump out front and behind that was a beat up shack propped with two-by-fours. On the roof a sign painted in drippy letters said "Cut Flowers." She grew her flowers in back of the shack and when you bought a bouquet out front you could see her mattress on the floor. Mom and pop always stopped there on the way to Cape May because she had beautiful snapdragons. But they never let me out of the car.

The Flower Lady smiled at me shyly from the couch. She was dressed in a clean white blouse and a hat decorated with real roses and had squeezed into tight jeans and white sandals.

Grandpop put his arm around her, lit up a White Ash cigar with one hand, leaned forward and asked "Know anything about giant fireflies?"

"Ahh," she said.

"Grandpop saw one once," I said. "He was playing his flute right here at the beach at dawn. The firefly swooped out of a cloud and almost swamped grandpop's kayak with the wind from its wings."

"Ahh," she said.

"It didn't mean any harm though," I assured her. "It was Horace."

"Quite a gentleman too," grandpop said. "He smiled at me to excuse himself. He uttered a few

118

unsonic words about the musical Kingdom of Firefly. He embraced me with his huge insect wings, the universal firefly embrace. Then he flapped off towards the horizon. I lost sight of his blinker in the rising sun."

There was a long silence. "Know anything about musical instruments dear?" grandpop asked, reaching into his vest pocket and producing his instrument.

"What's that?"

"The firefly flute."

"What do you do with it?"

"Why anything you like!"

"Grandpop invented it!" I explained.

"For what?" she asked, screwing up her face.

"It's got the most perfect pitch of any noise-maker ever crafted. With this instrument you can hit something that very nearly approximates the unsonic pitch of King Firefly. Scientists say firefly light gives off no heat, well their song gives off no sound," grandpop said, kissing the flute.

"Why would you want to sound like a bug?"

"To please him. Maybe one try, maybe another reaches him. You don't have much of a chance to do that with any other instrument, now, do you?"

"It took years to make the firefly flute," I pointed out.

"Years and years of testing, combining and tuning," grandpop added.

"It only plays one note," I said.

"Right."

"What good's one note?" she complained.

"You really want to see, luv?"

"I'm not sure."

"Well, if you plan to be my bride, you've got to learn about the flute," grandpop ordered. He helped her up and waved for me to follow.

He jumped down the porch steps and marched for the beach. It was pretty dark out because the moon was still behind the hurricane clouds, but the wind was quieter; some fog was settling into the dunes. The Flower Lady and I followed grandpop as he slogged through the sand, holding his hat on. All the cottages were black and some were already shuttered for the winter.

We dragged grandpop's kayak from under the boardwalk to the surf and unfurled the orange sail with the firefly emblem sewn on the peak. Grandpop left his boots standing on the sand and waded out, holding his flute high overhead to protect it from the spray.

Out beyond the breakers at waist depth, he laid the flute in the bottom of the kayak and climbed in and snatched up the sheet rope.

The Flower Lady shouted to him to be

careful. Grandpop waved back at her to be quiet. He sailed out a short ways into the calmer swells.

Presenting the flute to the darkness, he recited the magic crusade words that only he knew and we weren't supposed to hear. I thought I heard them, but I wasn't sure.

The flute shone in a shaft of moonlight. Its bell was hacksawed from a saxophone and the oboe stem was melted and yanked in a million bends. He put the flute to his mouth and blew the note, which none of us could hear, not even grandpop. The note was too holy.

It lasted until he ran out of breath. Then he looked out to the foggy horizon and waited.

When five minutes were gone, grandpop blew again. A jagged breaker dashed out of the water and almost spilled the kayak. He got his balance and yelled the magic words. I could almost hear them. He blew the silent note again. He waited.

"What's he waiting for?" the Flower Lady asked.

Grandpop sat in his kayak, repeated the words and puffed for another hour. Once I thought I spied a pale blinker moving just off shore and I pointed it out to the Flower Lady. Grandpop saw it too and hollered and danced around in the boat. "Over here! Here we are!"

The blinker began to dim in the fog. Grand-pop tried to charm it back with flute and words but it never formed again.

Grandpop sailed out of the ocean, banged the flute down in the hard wet sand and picked it up and banged it down again and again. He threw his hat in the air and went home.

The Flower Lady bustled off down the beach. After catching up with the hat, I chased her. "Please don't leave him! He hasn't got any-body!"

"Is your grandfather maybe crazy?"

When we got back to the house, grandpop was sitting on the floor with the flute in his lap, drinking out of an Old Mr. Philadelphia bottle, muttering and belching. He hollered his favorite poem by a Welsh poet, the poem that inspired him in the first place to invent the flute. He mo-tioned with his finger for the Flower Lady to come sit by him, but she shook her head and fastened one hand on the doorknob.

There was a squeak from the stairs. Grand-pop kept on reciting but you could tell from his eyes that he heard it.

Kathy ghosted around the corner of the stair-well. Grandpop tried to get to the end of his poem by keeping his eyes straight forward. Kathy glided into the center of the room in her white hospital gown and stood with her back to him, staring out the window at the faintly purple sky.

Grandpop stopped reciting. He looked at Kathy with tired eyes, choking and clearing his throat. He set his bottle aside and picked up the flute. Lifting his arms to Kathy, whispering the magic words, he blew the unheard note.

We all looked at Kathy. The Flower Lady stood with the door half open as the sky grew lighter and lighter.

Kathy turned without a sound, staring straight ahead wherever she turned. For a second she was staring right into grandpop's eyes and he into hers. Then she drifted towards the stairs and we heard the squeak again as she climbed back up.

Grandpop began to cry in big bursts. The Flower Lady slammed the door behind her. Through the morning mist I saw her white sandals flashing.

Grandpop stopped crying and lit up a cigar. Then he grabbed the flute and dashed a crooked hole in the tube, which exploded and chucked glass all over the room.

"Goodnight, grandpop."

"Goodnight, Kipper."

From my bedroom I could hear him smashing things downstairs. Now and then he quoted some of the Welsh poet. The sun came up and he cursed it and demanded the moon. The sun got hotter and brighter and he got madder and madder. He totaled all the furniture in the living room and ruined mom's favorite picture of Boston in a snowstorm and yanked the tablecloth from under the breakfast dishes. He plugged up the drain hole in the kitchen sink and opened the tap full blast. He made double sure there wasn't one windowpane left unpulverized.

He made a mistake in booting Willy though. Later, when they found grandpop asleep in all the mess in the bathtub, his foot was chewed. Willy's usually pretty nice, but he doesn't like to be surprised.

Grandpop was still passed out when they bandaged his leg and carried him to the gold van.

The tide poured over the bow. It rushed past and undermined the wet sand sides. I managed to save the anchor and paddles but had to abandon the rest of the kayak.

I turned my back and trudged off through the dunes.

I struggled to remember the magic words of the flyspec all the way home. I concluded he never said any words.

Like Uncle Charlie figured, grandpop was probably just a dipsomaniac—a guy who drinks too much and gets visions of insects.

Fourteen

"Comin' in Kipper," he shouted through the steel door this morning.

"O.K.," I said. I'm never too enthusiastic about seeing him.

I heard the clanking of his key chain as he unlocked the three locks. He usually talks to me through the talk-hole and has mail and parcels fed in through the revolving wall panel.

Ducking his head around the door, the chief checked me over with a fake smile. "Mornin' Kipper. We got something for you." He paraded in followed by two zombies packing revolvers and toting an exercycle. They set it down and went to guard the open door. Sure enough, it was a

125

Schwinn, the brand grandpop and I selected for the flying bicycle.

He slashed open a letter: " 'Happy fifteenth birthday and best regards, The President.' He sent you this for your health."

"Send him a thank you."

"Is everything in order?"

"Can I have the flute, maybe?"

Grinning sarcastically, the chief left with his two buddies.

Minutes later I saw Tania out the window, sort of parking her Jaguar in front of Liberty Bell Federal Savings. Her Secret Service man unpacked a crate of complexion soap while she skipped across the road for her second visit today. I'm glad the President gave me the exercycle: it will keep me in shape for his daughter. She's pretty nice, the best girl I know next to Kathy.

My only other visitor is Col. Cole. He strides through the door every day at four o'clock on the second. He drills me in math and strides out at four forty-five. The school board isn't paying him to tutor me but he figures it's his duty. He ignores me and looks through the window bars.

Every day a maid tidies up my bed and dumps my ash trays. She's also a spy, peeping in my pockets and under the bed, checking up on what the t.v. camera misses. She doesn't speak

English so hot so we have very little to say to each other. At meal time, she produces chow and plastic utensils through the revolving panel. Tania warned the chief that fried chicken and rice with raisins is my favorite, so I have it four times a week. Other days I devour lamb or steak or spare ribs. Now and then an admirer will mail me a fruit cake or salt-water taffy.

I make love to myself in a double bed that Mirabella would have dug and there's a leather chair that leans way back and vibrates. They pipe in violin music all day. The chief's wife gave me an old couch and the oriental rug and framed pictures of me from news media. On Wednesdays a guy comes to show me first-run Hollywood flicks, mostly tributes to the God of Death and Boredom.

I have no complaints except for six points. First, the double window bars are strictly ridiculous. I am *not* a threat to society. Second, besides Tania and Col. Cole I'm not allowed to receive visitors in my room; I take interviews through the talk-hole. Third, when I get out of here I'm raising a giant size stink about royalties for all the info I give out. Fourth, they won't lend me any books, even harmless fiction. The President backs up the chief on this. Fifth, I'm being held against my constitutional rights. They haven't even made up their minds what I'm here for!

The chief is the only one in the U.S.A. who thinks he knows for sure. "The kid has an anti-American mind," he snorts. He'd really like to cram me into a lobotomy machine. But he's got to maintain his cool if he wants the President to pose with him for pictures. The President says I just might be an important specimen and he wants me protected like some sort of redwood tree or whooping crane. I'm safe as long as the chief runs for mayor and gives a darn what the President thinks.

Most important is six: Tania tells me they're conniving to chop down Galápagos. This is just childish! What harm can a tree fort be? Maybe they're afraid the Democrats will declare it a historical monument. Today I'm whipping off a memo to the White House demanding that he proclaim an injunction or something. I'll send it through Tania since I don't trust the chief out of my sight.

I built Galápagos in a grade A tree, a hickory just outside my back yard near the radio tower. It was tall as a nine story building. I figured it sprouted when Washington was still a surveyor, because it took up the sun for an acre. Nothing could grow around it. Botanists called it a wolf tree.

I found out that hickories were so tough that rather than crack in a storm, they'd stand and take it until the ground gave out and let go of the roots. In fall, the leaves turned bright colors and hung on until spring.

I began constructing Galápagos just after I got home from Cape May.

Tooling up the driveway, I spotted pop jamming something into the incinerator. I oogaed and he jerked up, dropped the incinerator lid and stuffed like mad, burning his fingers, puffing sparks all over his suit, I threw a bucket of water on the fire.

But it was too late. In the ashes were the remains of my library, including the cloth cover of *The Budding Schemata* by Dr. Carlton Lampery with 1,400 charred pages. Dr. Lampery had predicted the male of the future will have a forehead camera lens to see with. His skin will be a layer of leaves and he won't have a mouth, because he eats by photosynthesis; or go to the john, because he transpirates. The female will be the same as the male, only she'll hang a grass skirt over her head with a hole to snap pictures through. They won't worry about sex because they'll use seeds and flowers.

"That does it, pop! I'm moving out! I'm building a fort, in the woods and you'd better keep out of my way!" I yelled, deciding to stow me and my books some place safer.

He wrung out his suit jacket and thought it over. "Kipper, I've prayed the Holy Ghost would give you an answer to your secular sickness.

Maybe a week in the woods would do it. He moves in mysterious ways," he said, retreating into the house.

"And you can double my allowance for the books," I hollered.

The first problem in building Galápagos was transportation one hundred feet into the treetop. In case of attacks, a wooden ladder would only give a boost to my enemies. During the noon lunch hour I lifted a roll of one-inch nylon rope from the Hardware while the clerk munched on a sandwich in the back. I felt sort of guilty at first; then I overruled myself with common sense.

I wove a ladder and tied it in the tree, dangling it for about seventy feet, using branches for the last thirty feet to the ground.

The skeleton was these eight five-by-six steel beams I uncovered in a stack of building materials at school and lashed to the hickory. On top of the bottom beams I bolted cedar planking. To pay for it, I borrowed gas from Mr. Pentapholis' Thunderbird.

He had his car rigged with an alarm, so I wriggled on my back underneath to snip the gas line. I borrowed fourteen gallons the first afternoon. He had just filled up. Later he rushed out of his house on the way to the trotters. The Bird whined and clunked. I sauntered over and asked him what seemed to be the trouble.

After I taxied him to the track in my car, he flipped me four dollars. When I met him late that night, he was falling down drunk from his Daily Double winnings. He slipped me a twenty-dollar bill and pinched my cheek. At home I siphoned him ten gallons from the Corvette and pretended it was on me. He said that I was a very noble youth and stuffed ten dollars into my pants pocket.

I was his helper whenever his car wouldn't start: mostly I disconnected his battery or fan belt. He pondered for a week and decided I was a genius mechanic.

For walls, I borrowed red and white fiberglass panels from Reverend Hocheisen's pool patio. For the roof, I requisitioned a red and white wrestling tarp from Col. Cole's back yard. It fit so snug I kept it for the duration. On a clear day I could see it all the way from school.

Around the base of the hickory, I designed a maze of upright logs, compliments of Bell Telephone. Only I knew the path through. I rigged a bed sheet sling for Willy. I hauled him up to live with me.

The rest of the stuff I lifted here and there along the Main Line.

The first night I emptied a can of Diet-Pepsi on the roof and dubbed my hideaway Fort Galápagos, after an island in the Pacific, raw and empty, a no-nonsense place just like the Fort. I shinnied to the top of the tree. I wired a lightning rod to the highest twig.

I regulated the Sterno heat in Galápagos at a steady fifty-five; any higher and I can't think. The chief has figured this out. He gets his kicks watching me sweat on closed circuit t.v.

After opening ceremonies, I let down the north wall so an icy wind whizzed in and kept my brain snapping. I had a front row seat to the universe; I felt I could twirl the galaxies around my big toe. All the way out, thousands, billions, trillions of miles into space, I tried to get to the bottom of it.

I meditated for three hours, sipping coffee, smoking Lucky after Lucky. When the time was up, I scotch-taped a new chart to the wall of Galápagos. Finally I understood Uncle Charlie.

THE WHAT WORKS WORKS CHART

I—GOAL

The purpose of the markings on this Chart is to get my face on the cover of *People* magazine or any other national publication by the time I'm nineteen. I am setting the date back because of the sluggish advances of the last few weeks while I labored under the millstone of the old Virtue Chart.

Method—What Works Works. Rating daily.

II—THREE SUB GOALS

Sub Goal One—Get Mirabella

Method—Any trick that works.
Addenda—Workable rules for love:
- A. When you laugh, show your teeth.
- B. Don't be wishy-washy and girl-like; be tough.
- C. In love matters, tenderness goes a long way.
- D. Listen to Mirabella; pay attention to her until you are enveloped in her presence.
- E. Lay off chocolate for your complexion's sake.
- F. Don't do C. T. because it ruins your love for her.
- G. Act as if you have 100 girl friends and couldn't care less about Mirabella.
- H. Do not giggle.
- I. Be yourself.

Sub Goal Two—Sainthood

Method—Find at least a few clues to the eternal way to live. Now! Proclaim these clues from the mountain tops, or at least from the radio tower. (Note—the words "a few clues" must not be taken as the maximum.)

Don't bother with the albatross of virtue.

Sainthood has got nothing to do with virtue: What Works Works.

The meditation period has been advanced from ten minutes per night in the alcove to three hours per night in Galápagos.

Sub Goal Three—Student Senate President

Method—Christmas Cards. Mail thousands to Grey Areas. They will believe it. There are more Grey Areas in the towers than lemmings in Lapland. The Grey Area is the normal voter, the basis of your power, the one with the radio plug in his ear. He who wants Everything must impress the Nothing. Sign card "I want to be your friend, Kip. Homeroom #288."

Above all, get cracking! You aren't growing any younger.

Fifteen

WHEN mom and pop were safely asleep in nightshades and ear stoppers, I let myself in the back door and lifted the keys to the cellar.

Filed in his Family History Achives I found the tape of grandpop's funeral party.

Up in Galápagos I threaded the tape on my portable recorder, singling out Uncle Charlie's player piano laugh to his girl. I tuned up on my trombone until I got my voice into his exact pitch. All morning I practiced running up the mechanical octaves of his laugh, taping myself and playing it back, until the tapes were twins.

I had already reconnoitered Mirabella's after-school habits. On the last whistle, she zipped down the temporary girls' elevator, cleaned out her locker in the empty locker room and waltzed to the bus: time lapse, three minutes twenty-eight seconds.

There were only three lockers in the new girls' locker room, surrounded by urinals from the time it was the boys' locker room. Behind the urinals, the wall had been bashed out and the pipes were bare. This would do for a staging area.

I made up my pimples and grabbed Uncle Charlie's red wig. I'd hid the wig inside Kathy's bowling machinery when he dropped it during his helicopter escape. The wig was the fail-safe joke.

I drove to school in time for the last class.

I watched the second hand on the homeroom clock drag to the end of the day. Col. Cole whistled in the amplifier: Mirabella wiggled to the elevator; I trotted along behind her. I reached around the elevator door and touched the forty-second floor button.

While she climbed, I charged to the Guidance Office, plunked down a nickel for a pink "Stamp Out Teenage Drug Abuse" balloon and charged for the hole.

I jumped to the basement floor and sprinted to the locker with Mirabella's gift bouncing along the ceiling pipes behind me.

Two steps ahead of the elevator's arrival, I was hidden sideways behind the urinal, stuffing the balloon under my shirt like mad. I tried to scrunch the wig on my head but it was too small. I'd have to balance it.

"It just isn't kosher when Peter and me had all that in common," Sharon Singer said as the elevator door rolled back.

"Sure, you're dying to see me get the same you got from Hunnicut," Mirabella said.

"Of course not, Mirabella. You're my best friend."

"Then lend me one until I can get to the drug store. Daddy took me last time and he'll be suspicious if I ask again tonight. Just one. Please?"

"I like Pete too much. I can't let you do it with him."

"You may like him but he told me he's had it with you! Put that in your pipe!" Mirabella yelled and slammed open her locker door.

"Think so?"

I heard paper being crinkled open.

"He didn't write that. Peter can't write, not that nice."

"Sorry. It's his handwriting. Looks like yours truly still has a piece of Peter."

"O.K. let him knock me up! Then see what you get of your good old Peter! Besides, if *I* decided to have an abortion, I'd be twice as popular as you!" Mirabella screamed.

If they started to gouge eyeballs, I wouldn't stand a chance. I stomped out of my staging area, balancing the wig and unleashing Uncle Charlie's trick in all three octaves. "Ha! Dough, ray, me, fah, so, la, tea, dough, etc. Surprise!"

Mirabella was screeching at Sharon and couldn't hear me. I stood between them like a goof with my eyes crossed and tongue hanging out.

"You've got the personality of a great auk!" Mirabella hollered at Sharon.

"You'd have to have ten abortions to be as popular as me!" Sharon screamed back.

I held the balloon out to Mirabella. She bent over and snatched her book bag from the locker. "Ha! Dough, ray, me, fah, so, la, tea, dough, etc. Surprise!" The wig slipped off. I trapped it against my nose and clamped it on again.

"Well at least he'd pay for *my* abortions. I wouldn't have to run to *my* daddy!" Mirabella blasted.

Mirabella glared at Sharon. Then her eyes seemed like she remembered something. She looked up at me. "What was it you wanted, Kipper?"

"See, I thought you might like this balloon to play with," I explained.

"I'm not a drug abuser, Kipper," she smiled.

"It's just a gift. Pink for girls, all that."

"Thank you, Kipper!"

"You're not making up to this jerk are you? Girl, are you hard up! He hasn't got *any* friends!"

138

Mirabella would get even with Hunnicut for that note. She'd go out with me and obliterate him with jealousy. I softened her up for the kill "Pink for girls! Ha! Dough, ray, me, fah, so. . . . "

St. George swooped around the corner in her "Happy Birthday Siva" cape. "You laugh like a tape recorder," she greeted me. "Dead."

"A tape recorder!" Mirabella screeched. "A dead tape recorder!"

Uncle Charlie's laugh fell apart in mid-octave. Sharon giggled; Mirabella snorted; then they howled until the basement echoed.

"Kip, don't play with these shallow nymphs!" St. George pleaded and hung on me.

I shrugged her off, whammed the balloon on a nail, and marched precisely all the way to the parking lot.

A block from home I hooked a left and down-shifted past the jail, oogaing, wolfwhistling, ding-donging and tooting Dixie. But they weren't interested.

I squealed around the block and tried again. But the cops weren't doing their duty, probably out campaigning with the chief.

"He could *not* be wrong. How could he be wrong?" I debated as I shifted for a third circle of the jail.

"He got rich! He got girls! He got on the cover of *Geriatrics Forum*! Maybe he even got away with murder! If he didn't know, nobody knows!" I figured out loud.

I wondered, "Maybe grandpop really knew magic words."

"Look where it got him" I answered.

I sat yoga in Galápagos, watching the sun set, while thoughts came at me in rushes. I decided for eight o'clock, half an hour before closing.

"This try you'd better be right! I haven't got time to mess around!" I told Uncle Charlie to myself.

As eight o'clock ticked closer, I worried if my hand would be too sweaty to hang on to the phone. At seven fifty-six I left Galápagos, drove to the phone booth and jammed my rally race driver's glove into my mouth. Her father answered, yelling over chattering voices. "Yeah?"

"Mr. Mason, like to speak to your daughter," I said, coughing up a glove finger.

"Think so?"

"Col. Cole here."

"So?"

"I'm your daughter's principal, sir. Put her on immediately."

I heard him yell the info at the butler. About ten minutes later Mirabella finally bothered to get to the phone. "Yes?"

"Mirabella, actually this isn't Col. Cole. It's a friend of a friend," I mumbled.

"Who?"

"Friend of a friend. Say how'd you like a ride in a new Corvette triple two barrel Sting Ray to the Sun Ray?"

"A Corvette sports car?"

"Sure."

"Who is this? How did you hear I need to go to the drug store?"

"ESP."

"Do you know Pete Hunnicut?"

"Friends from old times."

"You sure you got a Corvette?"

"Right. What time shall I pick you up?"

"Who is this?"

"What time?"

"Who *is* this?"

"Be practical, Mirabella. I have a Corvette. You need a ride."

"It's Kipper!"

I whipped out the glove. "Mirabella, listen! You and me make good practical sense!"

Her laughter was a sound like you get if you dial wrong.

"Mirabella, I'm going to be powerful and famous. I'm discovering the eternal. If. . . . "

"You sure are."

" . . . we get together. . . . "

She hung up.

I collapsed in the booth and thought about ripping the wires. But I didn't have time. The election was less than a week off and the Contest was closer than that.

"What kind of a jackass takes the advice of a murderer?" I asked myself, barrelling for home.

Sixteen

GRANDPOP'S trunk of G. A. leftovers sat in the attic where pop and Uncle Charlie had stashed it. Axing it open I found grandpop's hiking boots, Irish cape, walking cane and Halloween hat. I sorted through layers of tangled and broken puppets, a tube of Dentu cream, reading glasses, magazines on magic, and under everything two dozen bottles of Old Mr. Philadelphia Corn Meal Mash Spirits, some full, some half full, some empty. The spirits had leaked all over the book at the bottom, a copy of *Sonnets For An Unknown Firefly,* wrapped in brown paper and addressed to me.

Sonnets was grandpop's only published work. He paid a bundle to the Aphrodite Press to put it out and went around door to door, but he didn't sell one copy. He reviewed it gloriously under a fake name; nobody would print the review. Cartons of his poems wound up in our Cape May house, where I tried but was never allowed to read a copy.

I tucked the book in my pocket and footed it to Galápagos. Scooping up an old Cub Scout flashlight, my pipe and a fresh pouch of Prince Albert, I climbed as high above Galápagos as I could. I discovered a branch a little thicker than my thumb just below the lightning rod. Sitting there, I could stick my nose above the rod, making me the highest thing in that part of the state except the WHAA tower.

I named it "meditation roost," a great, deadserious spot where I had to cool it, smoke slowly and not think any wild thoughts that could dump me one hundred twenty feet past Galápagos into the maze. With *Sonnets* in my lap, pipe in my left hand and flash in my right, I opened to page one.

There was no page one! The centers of all the pages had been ripped out! The hollow was sloshing with Old Mr. Philadelphia Spirits.

I groaned and poured the booze into the air. A bunch of stuff tried to slip through my fingers: one, the firefly flute! two, a soggy envelope with something inside . . . a letter from grandpop!

144

"Salutations Luv,

I had to mutilate this last copy of my works, but I'm sure by now, if you ever get this, you've noticed the clever secret compartment. I'm wrapping this as Hymns of the New Order, so it might escape the fort censors. It's the only book I've managed to keep hidden. Your uncle thinks all copies are at the dump. He constantly investigates me. He has all these goats and nannies convinced I'm insane.

"This eon orgasm business . . . hard to stay awake. The fort's declared I'm aging unhappily; tomorrow they've slated me for Special Treatment in Orgasm of History. Tonight I bust out of here, past the saber-toothed hounds guarding the gravel wastes. If I don't see you again, you'll know I ended up as Kennel Ration.

"Don't unduly mourn the loss of me or the works. My day will return. At the end of this note I'll sum up with the magic words of the crusade that I promised you. If this doesn't make it to you, I'll try again through a spiritual messenger.

"The Firefly Kingdom is in temporary retreat. The forces of pragmatism, in league with sick righteousness, roll over the continents, trampling spirit into order. Long I've battled for spirit.

(ink smeared by booze)

"Your grandmother and I started as puppeteers, doing the children's birthday party circuit. Milly played Snow White, while I managed all

145

seven dwarfs at once. . . . Then t.v. and no more traveling puppeteer market.

"To support ourselves we were forced into the House of Sirloin, Inc.; Milly in beef bouillon; me as overseer of a demonic liverwurst machine with levers and gears grunting out hygenic, vitamin-fortified, ready-wrapped crap. Milly died; working, sleeping, working; then dead for real. I fought the House of Sirloin as best as I could. I winged among the slaughter-penned animals. We fed each other on promises of the spirit.

"Firefly told me about a cloud kingdom of bubbles and umbrellas, ruled by a Parliament of Passenger Pigeons, with a Judiciary of Dodos, Kinged by His Musical Majesty. I've longed to lift a glass with Firefly, singing his limericks; some day I'll be able to master his unsonic sounds.

"Grandson, in these pages I wanted to tell the world about the deep-down dwelling Spirit, rooted in the core of all living things. But the pragma-right public wouldn't let my foot in the door. . . .

(ink smeared)

"Pragma-right has a vacant gaze. Pragma-right builds freeways, super markets, crematoriums, bombs and boredom.

"Since 62,051 when Horace defeated darkness on the plains of Arkansas, the hour has never been so crucial. The King of Music, Light,

On-Going, Mad Laughter, Irreverence, and Contradiction must win.

"And that, grandson, leads to the words of the flyspec. Use it with care. I searched under millions of firefly clouds for this single dropping of Horace's. The flyspec commands. . . .

(ink smeared)

"Begin the crusade! Rally the universe to the cry of . . . (ink smeared)

So long for now, *Grandpop*"

No clue! I could hardly balance. No flyspec! All that searching destroyed by a few drops of Corn Mash. I stood up on the roost, shaking the letter at the cosmos. "Look here . . . " I started to yell.

I heard it crack. I flailed around my head for something to hang on. I came up with handfuls of dried leaves and nuts. The dead roost broke off and we nose-dived together, me making a swipe at everything with one hand, clinging to the letter with the other.

Falling.

Falling, I heard grandpop shout to me from that distant time, from that other fall. I was twirling like a maple seed, wings straight up, the bike dangling from my pant cuff. But I couldn't hear him.

Falling towards death, I thought of Kathy, like Sleeping Beauty, with no Prince Charming to kiss her awake. I thought of Mirabella smiling in my eyes and hooting. One vote lost for President of the Senate. She'd gossip—minus one hundred votes.

To Mirabella I was a nothing, a funny nothing. To the disappearing moon I was nothing, a relative rock. I shivered. A lot the burning stars cared if a nothing got any heat.

I was tumbling towards miles of frozen H_2O. Soon I'd be six feet under all that, with zero degree winds whipping over my bones, on their way to nowhere in particular.

Again I heard what sounded like grandpop's voice. But it vanished.

There was an awful stillness in the winter, a stillness that meant more than no sound. Cold, empty silence pressing down on me, Kip!

Crashing through the twigs, I rammed a finger into the evolving, spinning universe. "You can't ignore my death! I exist!"

I whacked my head on a branch. The moon and stars dimmed. "No universe is going to forget me! Kip! I am feeling stuff that can fill up any emptiness! I am! I am! I am!" I yelled at the galaxies.

But unfortunately I'm not sure I proved anything. I lost track of the whirling planets, lost track of what the whole point was in the first place.

As I plowed through the lower branches, I had a vision of St. George leaping in her sari.

Yup, she was right. All efforts to figure it out, even to stay alive, were hopeless. There was no use in fighting what must be.

I waited for the final revelation.

Seventeen

BUT his faint voice, calling from that other fall, years past, wouldn't let me go.

I was in grade school. Grandpop was over ninety. Fixing up the bike was grandpop's brain storm and he let me help him. Mom and pop wouldn't lend us the garage, so we staked out an orange tent in the back yard. We laid rolls of shelf paper on the grass floor and crayoned our plans full-scale.

When the diagrams were finished, I gave a report in science period, chalking the pedal-wing gear on the blackboard. The kids broke up; they stomped the floor and whistled. "You scientific apes!" I yelled. So the teacher made me sit down. A popular kid shoved me out of my desk and got away with it.

This was the first Schwinn in history with a goose-honk battery horn in the fat center post. Before that Schwinn bikes only had tinkling handlebar bells. Grandpop rode it to work at the meat factory until they fired him for talking to the animals. Then, for years he criss-crossed the U.S.A. from all angles, pedaling along, over mountains, through deserts, studying firefly clouds and searching for Horace's flyspecs underneath.

He became an expert on clouds from L.A. to Boston. He mailed essays to *The National Geographic,* but he never heard back from them.

When we found the bike under the porch, the tires were flat and the horn battery was dead, but the rest was o.k. In the tent, we stripped off the cowcatcher invention, headlight, noisemaker, fenders, chain guard, spinners, buffalo tails, orangutan hair saddle cover and chromium handlebars. We bolted on non-moveable aluminum handlebars. We unbolted the fat wheels and fastened on light racing wheels with helium-filled tires. After that I could lift the bike with a twig. All we left was the saddle, the basket, the goose-honk horn with a lifetime battery, the speedometer and a ten-second blinking flashlight.

According to exact proportions, measured from thousands of fireflies, grandpop calculated

I'd need seven feet of firefly shaped wing on each arm. Happy Farms was developing then, using sheets of aluminum in central heating systems. We hiked over and grandpop recited his poems. The workers grouched we could take all the leftover aluminum we needed if he'd lay off the poetry and let them get back to work.

For phase one of the flight we planned I'd hold out my supported wings in a glide position. After that I'd power it by kicking away the wing supports, setting the pedal-wing gear and pedaling. Grandpop rigged the gear so that at full pedal my wings would flap once every second and a half.

Grandpop said according to his calculations, I could count on a triumphant landing, but in case of an air pocket or a bird, he welded a battery-powered fan on the handlebars with the blades bent like a propeller. To the rear of the saddle he tied a helium bag attached to a cylinder that could pump the bag full in seconds. To overcome the weight of the fan and the cylinder, he filled the bag half-way before starting.

A few days before my ninth birthday, the Schwinn was ready to fly.

Grandpop, Willy and me wheeled the bike to the top of our Sacred Hill in Valley Forge, overlooking the Schuylkill. It was like a Walt Disney nature movie when the sky paled over the river. One bird chirped and the rest joined in until the whole dawn was filled with an audience of cheering birds.

Many clouds were glowing as white as the top of a just-poured glass of milk. One of these clouds held the Kingdom of Firefly. "Firefly! Firefly! Here's mud in your eye!" grandpop cheered.

It was about thirty degrees, I guessed. The ground was frozen solid like we wanted; a strong breeze drifted uphill for me to bank off of.

We took time to pick a likely cloud to aim at. The street lights flicked out. We knew we'd have to step on it before pop found the bike gone and called the cops. We hustled through a review of the flight plan. With wings clapped straight back, I'd churn down to the oak with the charcoal lightning scar. Provided my speedometer read at least forty-five by then, I'd snap my wings into the support struts and glide up the sunbeam highway, trying to spot the Kingdom. If I saw it, I'd kick out my supports, engage the p-w gear and flap on in. I'd ask anybody I met for directions to Cadenza Castle and deliver my gift to Horace. In no case would I dismount or fold up my wings or I'd drop through the clouds like an anvil.

I mounted the saddle and grandpop strapped my arms to the firefly wings and my Keds to the pedals. He protected my head with a leather football helmet from his sporting days.

For a take-off ceremony, grandpop ad-libbed

a poem at the glowing cloud we had picked. "Accepting this winking messenger and our tidbit. (I'm too old to come.) Besides you know damn well you owe *me* a visit!"

After taping paper American flags to the tip of each wing, he stowed the gift in the wicker bike basket—a volume of *Sonnets For An Unknown Firefly,* locked in a gold treasure chest. The chest was my gift, part of the Long John Silver pirate outfit I got one Christmas.

"Remember, Kip, be sure to hold your wings out when you get there. If you fall out of that cloud you're a goner."

"O.K.," I said, not a bit nervous. Grandpop knew what he was doing.

I folded my wings back, while grandpop checked the blinker and the p-w gear. He started pushing and running to the side until I got my balance. Willy yapped and loped alongside.

"Good luck, Kip!" grandpop puffed.

"See ya later alligator," I yelled over my shoulder. Tucking my head down like he told me, I pedaled with long racing gear strokes. My wings slapped tight together in the growing wind. Willy barked encouragement next to me until he couldn't keep up.

The speedometer said twenty a quarter of the way downhill. The lightning scar loomed closer and closer. I didn't think I was going to make forty-five in time.

I pedaled so hard I swear the tires smoked in the cold air. Twenty-five, thirty-five, forty, the scar and bingo! I feathered. The supports held. The wings caught the uphill breeze. The tires danced above the rough ground. I was air-borne!

I heard grandpop's "hot damn!" behind me. I was gliding up the highway with the firefly cloud dead ahead. In a few seconds I'd investigate the top. I swooped a left turn over Happy Farms, gaining altitude.

The sunbeam highway leaped into my eyes.

Looking down to kick the p-w gear in place, I saw the elementary school. My right knee moved to the goose-honk button and I blew it at the school, knocking out the wing supports. I should have started pedaling immediately, but I was concentrating on the school. When I let up on the button, the horn stuck.

In that second, I lost altitude. The wings smashed straight up. I pedaled in panic. The p-w gear was no darn good with the wings overhead and I was falling too fast to pull them down.

With my teeth, I clicked on the battery fan, which slowed the front of the Schwinn, but the back fell at the same speed so that I was closing in on Happy Farms at a forty-five degree angle.

I heard grandpop shouting the words.

"Maybe he's telling me to inflate the bag," I thought, flipping on the cylinder switch with my knee. All I got was hissing.

Grandpop yelled again, the same magic words. Trying to get rid of the bike, I booted away the pedal straps. The bike fell with me until I shoved it down with my foot. My pant cuff snagged in the chain.

I stuck out my wings as best as I could, falling like a maple seed, spinning round and round.

I crashed in Reverend Hocheisen's partly frozen pool and bloodied my nose; but I managed to rip the bike off my cuff and prevent drowning. The Reverend was very upset and he fished me out and bundled me up and gave me hot cocoa and stuff while we waited for the ambulance.

On the way to the hospital, grandpop cursed and cursed. "We'll get there yet, Kip. This summer, you wait," he promised. But that was the summer mom and pop committed him to the Golden Age, because he was a dipsomaniac.

Lying in the snowbank at the foot of the hickory, my head blasted and my nose bloody, I suddenly heard his words plain. "Keep Up Your Spirits," grandpop had shouted.

Eighteen

Now my landing jarred pop's disaster alarm system. Searchlights glared off the snow; the burglar brain curdler wailed so loud that it set off alarm systems up and down the block. In the distance I could hear the chain reaction growing into one huge scream.

Police and firemen swarmed down our street, sirens competing for decibels. The yard was soon jammed with men in bathrobes and ladies with wrinkle-creamed faces.

Pop shut off the curdler and minced out into the snow. "Is that you, Kipper? I hope you're not doing anything too rash. Did you do that?"

Covering my ears, I lay in the snowbank for ages and thought about grandpop. "It was like he was John the Baptist, who thought up the crusade but was too far out about musical insects and things. He needed somebody with political ability."

By the time the neighbors had turned off their alarms and the authorities had snooped around the block, a foggy sun was squatting on the roof peak. My nose had quit bleeding.

I stalked through the trees, making sure mom and pop were back in the sack. I let myself in the kitchen and picked up two rolls of contact paper, scissors, Magic Marker and a double thick Acme bag. I phoned teenage radio WHAA and told them my brain storm, emphasizing it was a today only sign-up.

In the living room I fished *Semper Fidelis* from pop's collection of marches. I also borrowed his portable record player and loaned myself some cash from his desk. Up in the bedroom, I gathered fake parchment paper from the old Long John Silver kit. I climbed the attic ladder and stuffed the bag with grandpop's Halloween hat, his hunting cape, and the fold-up Felt Board.

I had the whole morning in Galápagos.

I snipped three hundred round signs out of mom's kitchen contact paper and printed on each one with red Magic Marker, *"PEP!"*

At the top of the four parchments I composed the Preamble to the Petition: "We the undersigned advocates of the spirited approach to life do hereby petition Col. Cole, Principal, and the School Board for a two hundred piece all-girl marching band and a boy drum major.

"Signers of this petition will be members of the Cheering Club.

"We thank Col. Cole for his cheerleading all these years but we respectfully ask his retirement and take over by the students."

I left room underneath for two hundred fifty numbered signatures.

On the Felt Board, I spelled out the aims of the Club, plastering a *"PEP!"* sign at the top. I switched on the recorder and erased every note of Uncle Charlie's laugh. In its place I recorded my voice repeating what was on the Felt Board, yelling it over and over, using the whole reel. "Free Tootsie Roll! Sign Up With Cheering Club! Pom Pom Girls! Majorettes! Girls' Marching Band!" I left out the boy drum major bit since I didn't exactly need competition.

It was 11:45. The lunch period started at 12:14.

I pulled on grandpop's moon hat and cape and tucked the firefly flute in my back pocket. Stuffing the rest of the gear in the Acme bag, I shinnied out of Galápagos and ran to the Corvette. On the way to school, I squealed into a candy store and stocked up with ten boxes of penny Tootsies.

Starting at 11:51, I covered the towers with as many of the three hundred *"PEP!"* posters as I could slap on the ceilings, floors, walls, windows, doors and the bulldozer parked in the hall outside the cafeteria.

At 12:14 I had set up a table from two sawhorses and a board and had laid out parchments, pencils and Tootsies. I had erected the Felt Board. I had turned on the Sousa march. I posed on the tread of the bulldozer, my finger resting on the "Play" button of the tape recorder.

I remembered the Felt Board lesson from years ago in the snow; lonely Jesus wandering in the felt synagogue, not even a teenager yet, just beginning to dream. "What a risk!" I told the kids. Jesus must have thought the rabbis would hoot at Him and chuck Him out on His ear. But, I had reminded them—flipping to a scene of Jesus teaching the teachers—never give up the ship. If you're not gutsy enough to stand four-square for your principles you'll never get anywhere. The final display was His mom and pop finding Jesus in the temple and shouting His hosannas. Of course, it was all a myth, I reminded myself.

At Col. Cole's tweet I pressed the button. For realism I pretended to be playing the firefly flute swinging my torso and bouncing my head like a determined marcher. They weren't a bit interested. As soon as the lead runner entered the hall, I knew it was trouble. The kids were insane with hunger. Somebody caught a leg of the Board and it collapsed on me. I flattened myself against the bulldozer as the hall filled with stampeding boots, followed by the gasps of losers with their winds knocked out and the whoops of winners standing first in the platter line. Over it all shrilled Col. Cole's whistle. He plunged past, reaching for the collar of a seventh grader. The kid squirmed through the legs of the mob jammed up at the door and disappeared into the cafeteria, leaving Col. Cole frozen with his hands out. He whirled and whistled inches from my face. "What's this?"

Coolly I turned off the tape and music. "Sir, I'm forming a Cheering Club to help school spirit, so we'll win lots of sports events. The Club could visit wounded vets and the Home For Incurables."

He considered me. A late girl ripped down the hall with her lunchbox in a pumping hand. He leaped, lashed out and got the box in a splatter of egg salad. Finally, he captured her at the Cold Milk stand. I watched him settle down at the faculty table and forget me for a bowl of peaches and wheat germ.

Through the glass partition I checked on who Mirabella was sitting with. As head of the Nominating Committee she'd already made sure

Hunnicut would be on the presidential ballot. I discovered her with Hunnicut. He was breaking all the rules. He was supposed to eat on the Shop L shift.

Col. Cole stopped munching long enough to whistle the end of the shift. In a few minutes, the kids got up and wandered out, weighted down by their full stomachs. After straightening the parchments and pencils, I rolled the sound effects and leaned against the dozer, blowing into the firefly flute.

A Grey Area stopped. The others saw him signing. They listened, read the Felt Board and signed up quick. I kept one eye to the ceiling, like I was concentrating hard on the march, and the other eye on the Tootsies.

"When's this so-called Club gonna meet?" a Grey Area asked when I refused him two Tootsies.

"The date's not set yet," I said, waving him along.

"What's your name? You dress like a fag!"

"Kip."

"You the one sent me the special delivery Christmas card?"

"Yup."

In a few minutes I had almost one hundred signed up.

I observed Mirabella leaving her table as Hunnicut carried their trays to the dirty dish room. Clicking off the sound, I folded the Board, stuffed the parchments under my cape and stood facing the wall. Some kid wanted to sign up but I ignored him. It had to be just me and Mirabella. When I thought she'd be in front, I whirled. "Hey, Mirabella!" I hollered down the hall.

They turned sort of casually. "I've got something for you to read. It's a new idea of mine!" They yukked a lot, but came back, Hunnicut held the parchment for Mirabella. "It's already the biggest club in school!" I pointed out.

"Where'd you get that nice hat?" Hunnicut sneered.

"I inherited it from my grandfather."

"What are you doing this for?"

"For everybody. For good school spirit. We've got to keep up our spirits and . . . "

"And what do *you* want out of it?"

"Nothing!" My darn voice squeaked.

"A date with Mirabella?" Hunnicut smiled.

"Maybe he'd rather be President of the Senate," Mirabella said.

"Or drum major." Hunnicut hooted.

Mirabella selected a Tootsie, gobbled it, stole another and pranced away with Hunnicut, ho-hoing deep in her throat.

I lay down on the tread and twirled the half moons, thinking there was something about the ho-ho—mocking or planning? I counted it planning. Mentally I marked plus one hundred.

They began to pass before I knew it, the Shop L shift, some slobbering or picking their noses; one with his fly partly unzipped. A few gibbered at private jokes. Most were silent, staring down at their lunch bags.

I could have let them pass. They never would have seen me. Instead, on instinct, I bounded up to the steel seat. "Hey looky here! A new club! Pep! Free candy if you join!" I waved my hat, tooted silently and danced.

Something about me thrilled them. Their mouths dropped open and they gaped up like I was a wizard. "Make your X! Pick up a Tootsie! Make two X's and get two Tootsies!"

Slowly they began to sign, chewing their Tootsies and signing up again and again. "Spirit! Spirit! Keep Up Your Spirits!" I yelled. One began to clap, taking care to make sure his hands met. Soon they were all applauding for me in the same slow rhythm.

A girl with gooey mascaraed eyes circled her hand, inviting me to come down and join them. Holding the cape like a parachute, I leaped from the seat to the floor. "Good! Wow!" they babbled.

"Come on gang! Show those in-kids our pep!" I yelled. I flounced out the cape and high-stepped down the hall. I listened to them sloshing behind me in time to the firefly flute. We crossed the foggy soccer field towards the Memorial Tombstone where I planned a proclamation.

"Kipper! Kipper! Wait up!" It was Mirabella, galloping across the lot, her hair flying. "I've been looking all over the towers for you! Where you been?" she puffed and frowned. "You still doing this club thing?" She suddenly smiled.

"Yes, the Cheering Club. It's sort of a spirit crusade."

"It sounds super, Kipper! I mean we girls would love being majorettes. Do you think Cole will dig the short skirts?"

"If these signatures mean anything," I said, rattling the parchments.

"Got a pen?" she asked, grabbing the bottom one. She kneeled on the asphalt and signed it on her bare knee.

"Tell you what, Kipper, if you keep me in mind for head majorette, I'll date you tomorrow night. What say?"

When she kissed me I got chocolate stuck on my cheek and lost my words.

Nineteen

"**D**EAR Teenager:

"We are delighted to inform you that your proposed exhibit in the National Teen Scholar Contest, Junior High School Department, has been approved by the Contest's Panel of Selectors. You are hereby permitted to enter your Local Contest. If you are successful there, have your Exhibit ready for the Federal Inspector in no later than ten (10) days.

"May we take this opportunity to wish you all the best of luck. We hope we will be able to welcome you to Washington for the National Award Ceremonies.

Bureau of Control"

The letter arrived Saturday morning. But as much as I had to come up with a brainstorm, I couldn't think about the contest. I spent the afternoon in Galápagos, imagining quiet beaches and peaceful meadows, trying like crazy to calm down. But the closer my date came, the worse my stomach felt.

About seven I ran down to the house to see if pop was ready to drive: kids my age weren't allowed on the roads after sundown and I didn't want Mirabella to figure me for a lawbreaker. But pop was just finishing his tapioca.

In the bathroom upstairs I made up my pimples and combed my sideburns and brushed my suede boots and puked in the toilet. Recuperating on the toilet seat, I tried to list on my fingers the rules for getting Mirabella to like me. I couldn't come up with one.

On the underside of my shirt cuff I wrote "Keep Up Your Spirits,!" and sketched topics of conversation: about the U.S. refusing to send any more food to India; about the cult of men and women living in the Pocono Mountains and refusing to pay any attention to each other.

When I jumped down the stairs, I found pop at the dining room table fiddling with his flash and cramming film into his camera. He wanted to photograph my first date.

Mirabella lived near Valley Forge on a cliff carved out by the Ice Age glaciers. The cliff leaned out over the Expressway, so high you couldn't hear the noise of the traffic. At the end of her driveway, a guard cranked down a crossing bar and checked us over. He telephoned the house and raised the bar.

I rang the Westminster Chimes until Mirabella lifted an upstairs window and waved and called down that I should open the door and wait inside. I stood in the hallway, fixing my sideburns by the reflection in the horn of a stuffed rhinoceros. A brass sign under the rhino said "Souvenir of Ebenezer's Butte Top Clinic."

Mirabella looked fine when she bounced down the stairs wearing a red, white and blue t-shirt. She handed me her coat and after a few swipes I managed to jam her arm into the sleeve. She smiled in my eyes while I did up the buttons.

Before I could get to it, she skipped to the car door. On the way to the movie theater I smiled at the side of her face, trying to get my spirits up. She stared past the guard and we drove for miles and I couldn't come up with a darn thing to talk about. "Did you see the article in the National Geographic about sacred cows?" I asked, polishing off my first cuff topic.

"Cows?" she said, like she smelled an odor.

"In India. All these cows are running around eating up the food and the people are starving. The holy men won't let them kill the cows because they're sacred. So the United States has cut off food supplies until they kill the cows."

Mirabella didn't know how to approach that: "You doing a geography paper on this?"

"No. I just read about it."

She looked at me for the first time; it seemed in her eyes like she hadn't caught the punch line yet.

"I'm really sympathetic about the cows," I said, feeling The Hand at my throat. I'd thought I left that behind in virtuous days.

"My leper committee sends them a lot of stuff," she said and turned away.

"Holy men fight off the foreigners that destroy the spiritual ideas that give meaning to their lives."

"So I suppose you think the U.S. should just let those cows take over?"

"On the one hand there's the need to eat, on the other the need for sacred cows."

"You sound like a professor, Kipper," Mirabella said after mulling it over.

"See," I was beginning to feel the spirits; The Hand let go my throat "In America we've got tons of food but we've exterminated our sacred cows. We're sitting here in the night after dinner surrounded by the corpses of all these cows and that's why Americans aren't satisfied and are committing suicide and taking drugs."

"Did you say something like that on the Petition?"

"What petition?" pop asked.

"The spirit petition! Oh boy, Kip's pop, you've got a famous son here. The word is all around school. He's founded a pep club to keep up our school spirits."

"Kipper is the Ultimate Heir too," pop said.

"I think that's nice, Kipper. Did you know that power leads to evolutionary advances in the personality?" Mirabella asked.

"Yes."

I had scored a lot of points so far and I didn't want to get into any arguments. I could sense in the air how happy pop and Mirabella were, feeling like it was just us three superior ones against all the outside.

The theater was holding a cowboy revival festival.

"Torture Plateau" blinked in purple lights. Pop left the engine running while he unloaded his gear, set up the tripod on the sidewalk and asked Mirabella and me to stand to one side of the neon sign. Walking back and forth with his light meter, he adjusted his exposure and told us to stand closer together so he could squeeze everything in.

"Come on pop, the movie's starting."

"Snap a few more, Kipper's pop. Please won't you?" Mirabella smiled sweetly. She snatched onto a telephone pole, flinging her head back and rubbing her mastodon hips against the pole. She wriggled in front of a movie poster with her hand in back of her head. "Get this," she said, posing on a fire hydrant and flipping her regenerated Idaho hair around.

"Naa," pop said when Mirabella danced over to me and fastened her arms around my waist. He packed up and came back to pay for the movie. "Be good, Kipper."

I waved him away and rushed into the darn theater, stumbling around in the dark, fifteen minutes late.

I decided to be a fan of the Cisco Kid and his buddy Pancho. After their first t.v. re-run, it was because they sided with H. G.'s forces against all odds. Now I decided it was because they kept up their spirits.

The Apaches trapped Cisco and slung him over a horse and carted him around for days and nights, with some beautiful photography of the desert. They staked him spread eagle on a plateau in the sun, trying to toast out the secret of the stored cavalry rifles.

I coughed once and raised my arm and winged it over Mirabella's head. My elbow smacked her plastic forehead. "Sorry," I apologized. When I wrapped my arm around the back of her chair, she grabbed her knees and leaned forward for the rest of the movie. My arm went to

171

sleep. Kids threw pennies from behind and they clattered on the floor.

"Kipper, take your arm down. It doesn't look right," she complained at the torture scene. The director had the Indians use modern psychology. "Pancho is a chicken, Pancho is a chicken," they chanted by tom tom beat all night long. They pretended that Pancho had been sneaking around with Cisco's girl friend and had been bribed in gold to set up the trap. But each time one of the redskins said "Pancho is a chicken," Cisco whispered "Pancho is a bull" and fixed his eyes on a firm desert star. That's how he kept his cool and hung on to the secret of the rifles and gave salvation to hundreds of white men. At sunrise, in rolled the cavalry with the bugles and the whole works and the Indians were either shot or hightailed it. Heading up the troops was fat Pancho and beside him was Cisco's girl, who smooched Cisco and bawled.

The lights flicked on and I gave a round of applause. Mirabella stood up, looking down at me like I was odd. The others wandered out in a stupor. I quit clapping since anyway my arm had gone to sleep and tingled and hurt.

"I wanna go to the Doomburger," she said.

Doomburger Heaven was jammed when we walked in. An integrated bunch of Shop L guys messed with the juke box, in foul moods because it was Saturday night and they didn't have the intelligence to think up something to do. The sight of me with Pete Hunnicut's girl didn't make them any happier.

I found a booth in the dark at the rear. Mirabella was upset to have been maneuvered into a position where she couldn't see the action; she kept standing up and craning her neck around. I didn't know what was so hot about a bunch of low I.Q's sprawling over a juke box but it was o.k. by me since I'd run out of things to say: I couldn't remember any of the topics scribbled on my cuff and I didn't want to get caught checking it. She got bored with the juke box and turned face to face with me. The Hand was at my throat.

I smiled at her in the theory that this might get something started. But it was no go. I looked at the floor, the tables and the walls. Mirabella's eyes seemed about to shut completely. I whammed the pepper grinder on the table. She woke up and scanned the menu, which was some stupid thing decorated with gigantic turtles. Dropping the grinder, I crawled under the table to retrieve it and tried to read my cuff in the dark next to Mirabella's legs. She lifted the tablecloth. "What are you doing under there, silly?"

"Putting the pepper back in the grinder," I said, scuttling out backwards into the chubby waitress, who had arrived to take our order. "Two double cheese pizzas with anchovies, sardines, and herrings," Mirabella ordered for us.

"That movie was so bad it was kicks," she said after our order arrived.

"Why do you say that?"

"The cowboy was a gas."

"Well I think some Westerns have a meaning besides being entertaining. Here's this one man, all alone in the middle of the desert and these redskins are conniving to reduce his spirits to chaos, back to the savage state they live in. But he refuses to crack. It's men like Cisco who are keeping up our spirits and preventing the human race from going back to the Indians."

"Eeeohhwow! You're right! Back to the Indians!" She was off in this dog whistle pitched laugh.

I figured lucky break number one. "No siree, Mirabella, he won't let us go back to the Indians."

This was good for three repeats until it wore out. She dabbed at her eyes and gave a slightly annoyed stare. My jokes had used up half the pizza.

"You're so right, Kipper. I'll bet you're too much at parties with that sense of humor. Do you like parties?"

"Some of them. I had an idea for a political party."

"I do too! But sometimes I go back to the Indians at parties. Were you at Pete Hunnicut's last bash? Petie and my parachute instructor and I stole a car, a Porsche even! We drove by

Lazar's Beer Distributors and boosted half a keg of Colt 45. It was the first Colt I'd ever had. I was gone, gone, gone. I hopped on my instructor's Harley-Davidson and crashed through a neighbor's fence and belly-wopped into their swimming pool and totaled the bike! I think I wanted to be a minnow again. Booze does that to me. . . . "

I had a few objections to raise on a moral point, like not destroying private property.

But I remembered the albatross Virtue Chart and where that got me. Besides Mirabella seemed to think I was a good listener. More touchdowns for my side.

"The neighbor gave us a big speech, said our lives were amoral, said we'd end up in reformatories," Mirabella said, ripping the menu to shreds. "Kipper, you're sort of a thinker. Is life more than forward or backward?"

"Yes," I said, leaning to her.

"What *is* a moral anyway?"

"My grandfather said to go on a spirit crusade."

"I think about morals sometimes. And do you know what I enjoy most of all?"

"What?"

"Dancing."

"That's no moral!"

"Yup. I'd do anything to be able to dance and dance and dance with my new body. In fact, know what?"

175

"What?"

"I invented a whole new step called The Greenpeace. Want to see?"

Before I could grab her, she was leaping around with her Mountain Dew in one hand and the remains of her pizza in the other. All these lunatics were ogling her! I couldn't have handled more than five of them without my cape and Tootsies.

Once in a while she stopped, jutted her hips forward and rotated them slowly. While the moron's eyes popped out, she ran her tongue over her mouth and rubbed her hands up her revamped body. She lay back over a table.

The owner shut off the box. "That's all, Miss. We don't allow dancin' on the premises, no license you know," he smiled.

Mirabella smiled back and skipped to the booth. "Like it?" she panted, wet with sweat. I offered her my handkerchief. "You do it, Kipper." I mopped off her face and neck for her, which upped my spirits.

"Kipper, remember back in Neighborhood Church . . . when we were together in Sunday School . . . Reverend Hocheisen said our bodies are the temples of God? Remember?" she puffed, as I folded in the wet part so my suit wouldn't get stained.

"I guess."

"Isn't that super . . . even if it's just a dream. . . . Doesn't it give you a surge!"

"Something like that."

"You know if Jesus does come again, guess what I'm going to do with Him."

"What?"

"Dance with Him! What rhythm He'll have!"

Pop picked us up a few minutes later. Mirabella leaned her head on my shoulder and listened to a radio revival program. A fast speaking convert predicted the world would burn up inside of three days and Jesus would arrive on clouds of glory.

I wondered if it was right to kiss good night on the first date: I'd never kissed any girl but Kathy. The guard stopped pop with the crossing bar. "O.K., George," she waved. We drove to the house and I escorted her to the front door where she slunk into a shadow and dug her hand down the neck of her t-shirt. "Think you can come on over in the vette later? We'll watch t.v. I'll tell Georgie to take the night off. Mommy and daddy won't be back from Jamaica for a couple of days?" She came up with a key.

When pop got me home, I said good night and trudged off toward Galápagos, hiding in the maze until I saw the lights flick off and then hustling down to the garage and easing up the door without the electronic eye. I shoved the vette out backwards and jumped in, letting it roll down the driveway.

The bar was up when I got to Mirabella's house. Except for a spooky glowing from some second floor window, the house was black. I parked next to the tennis courts and, jingling the door key on its chain, I walked to the front door, unlocked it and climbed the stair carpet.

"In here, Kipper."

I followed the voice and opened a door to the glowing room. She wasn't there. "Sit down and have the beer I opened for you. The can's on the table next to the Relaxicizor," her voice said from a wall intercom.

When I sat down, the darn thing immediately reclined and vibrated. "How do I turn off this chair?"

"The button on the side, goofy," the intercom said.

"Where are you?" I asked, hunting for the button I never found.

"In the bathroom getting ready. Don't get too bombed."

"I don't drink," I said, but I took a few swigs for politeness. The wallpaper was the school colors, red and white, in wavy stripes. One wall was plastered with about a thousand Yale, Princeton, State College, Army, Navy and junior and senior high school pennants. Filling the gloom behind me was a glistening pyramid of beer cans.

Mirabella's dresser was smothered with tons of special formula perfumes, lipsticks and cold creams. There were deodorants and mouth-washes from Pocatello and a bottle of Boise rare dew hair elixir; standing in back was a tin of Chimpanzee hormone. I decided I was going to find out more about her disease.

The furniture was occupied by an evolution of stuffed animals. A ten-foot-long tiger stared at me from the foot of her round bed, which was cir-cled by a smiling boa constrictor in red and white stripes to match the wallpaper. A real rose lay on the pillow and the flowered satin sheets were turned back.

The Hand grábbed at my throat. The longer she puttered in the john, the tighter It squeezed.

"Hide your eyes a minute," her voice said on the intercom.

I did and heard her swishing around the room. Violin music seeped out of the walls. "Okey dokey, you can look now."

Next to the bed squatted two iron toads with smoking sticks hanging out of their mouths. "You like the scent?" her voice asked.

"Hey, Mirabella, you said we'd watch t.v."

Her pink phone was off the hook. After ages her voice said "Ready?"

"For what?"

"For grooving, of course!"

She banged open the bathroom door in a

swirl of sweet smelling smoke, planning it so that the light was directly behind her and I could see her silhouette through the pink nightie, cut away here and there. I could see even better now what a great job the doctors had done. For the life of me, I couldn't remember my questions about her disease.

Calm as a cloud, she wiggled into the room on high-heeled slippers. "Here Abdul," she ordered. A live ferret wiggled from a pile of stuffed animals and snuggled into her arms. "He's usually tolerant," she explained, carrying the ferret to a purple cushion next to the Budweiser pyramid. "Sleep here and don't be lonely. Mommy still loves you."

Where she walked across in front of me was a Gulf Stream of perfume. "Last time I cheated on Peter, Abdul knocked down the cans. Abdul doesn't dig state college boys," she said, flopping on the bed. "Kipper, be a darling and come on over," she giggled and flexed her little finger.

With what was left of my spirits, I heaved myself out of the chair. I stumbled across the room. She pulled me down on top of her, forcing her tongue through my lips. "Let's Kipper, let's."

"What?"

"Take off our vines."

"You already got most of yours off."

"I'm embarrassed to be naked if you're not."

I worked on the top button of my shirt but with my shaking hands I couldn't budge it. Mirabella reached up and helped while digging into a box of Saran Wrap by her bed.

"What's that?"

"A little gift. I couldn't get to the drug store, remember?" she cooed, wrapping me up. "How come baby's thing is all wilted?" She yanked me on top of her again.

"I'm too heavy," I mumbled into the perfumed pillow. "I'll hurt you. I'm over seven foot tall."

"That's why it's so groovy. I knew you'd have a bigger one. If it wasn't all dangly."

I rolled off her. "I can't do it. It's against the Commandment."

"What Commandment?"

"Seventh."

"What's *that* say?"

"Thou shalt not commit adultery."

Mirabella laughed a short version of her dog whistle. "Another one of your morals. Adultery's for married people!"

"That's not what my pop said, I know virtue is a hoax but pop said if I mess with sex I'll go blind and deaf and all my hair will fall out.

"Eeeohwow! Your pop's off his rockeroo! I've done it lots, for each one of those beer cans in that pyramid! Is all my hair falling out?"

"Now it's not."

"Look, Kipper, what about if I nominate you for President of the Student Senate?"

I thought it over.

I stood up, ran across the room and pounced on her. Mirabella whined and thrashed, using up her hormones. I was afraid one of her replacement parts would come loose. Maybe she'd fall apart entirely. Then I stopped caring. . . .

I rolled off and relaxed with the Saran Wrap sticking up. Mirabella nuzzled against me while I checked her over. I was relieved to find out she was still in one piece. At first she smooched my neck fast and nibbled my ear, murmuring "I dig you, Kipper" slower and slower until she slept with her open lips against my neck and her arms around by big stomach.

I lay awake, starring at myself in the ceiling mirror, thinking about a lot of things, like what I was going to do for the Teen Scholar Contest in the next twenty-four hours.

I nudged Mirabella. She was smart, got good grades; even if she was a little nuts, I hoped she'd give me a clue. But she mumbled angrily. When I tried a second time, she bit my neck and hung on like a shark. I decided not to try her again, not while she was in a subconscious state anyway.

Then, for the first time, I thought about Kathy

and how we used to hold each other. But it seemed too drastic . . .

Sometime after five o'clock, Abdul the ferret clawed onto the bed and tried to fit between Mirabella and me. I couldn't unfasten her from my neck. So Abdul pulled out a key beer can and the whole sheebang clattered down.

Mirabella woke up and tried to roll me on top of her again, but the ferret beat me to it.

I dressed and tiptoed down the stairs.

At the peak of the Sacred Hill, the dawn was just beginning. I reached up my hand, groping for grandpop's hand somewhere in the universe.

Twenty

LATER I stationed Willy outside the empty house. Mom and pop had left for a suicide viewing at the Neighborhood Church.

Kathy lay in the grey light of the bowling alley. I clapped my hands in front of her eyes; she didn't blink. The cat scurried off the bed to hide under the bowling alley sheets.

Since they wouldn't do for the Fair's judges, I stripped off Kathy's hospital gown and rubber panties. Packed in the cedar chest, I found her cowgirl costume with the ten gallon hat, suede jacket and skirt with rawhide fringes, metal spurred boots and two genuine leather thigh-tie holsters and six shooters that popped wooden bullets.

After dressing Kathy and bundling her in blankets, I sat her on the passenger seat of the vette and dashed back into the house to collect all the framed pictures and photo albums of me that were not stored in the Archives. I picked up the experimental gear and a shotgun from pop's Disaster Kit and I stored them in the trunk.

I slapped Kathy hard three times to make sure, but she still didn't blink. Her head rested on the whiplash guard and her eyes stared up at the stars. I slapped her because I love her, I mean it wasn't any time to get sticky about stuff like that.

I rolled the trash barrel from the garage and set it on Kathy's lap and then I drove across the back yard to Galápagos. With the barrel wrapped in Willy's sling, I placed the photos and gear and Willy and Kathy in the barrel and hauled them up. I screwed eight screw eyes on the door and its frame, shut the door and snapped on four padlocks.

I opened a pack of penny lollipops and tried to get Kathy to lick up energy for the ordeal ahead at the Fair, but she didn't even wiggle her tongue.

Until ten o'clock I snipped enough pictures

out of the albums to fill half the trash barrel. I probably didn't need the pictures or the posters and stuff. After my victory at the Teen contest, I'd win the election hands down anyway.

I pinched Kathy. She didn't blink. Lying flat on the cot, she stared at the tarpaulin. I unsnapped the locks, lowered Willy in the barrel and zipped to school.

The three towers were dark.

With the bottom of the barrel, I busted a window in the girls' gym. It was graveyard quiet in the basement of the tower. From the tools scattered around I picked out a hammer for protection. Willy stuck close by my side as I crept through the basement and up the ladder.

I decorated the ninth grade tower first, digging into the barrel and Scotch-taping photos all over the walls. It didn't make any difference what age or pose I was in the picture. It was all me. There was one of me with grandpop and the Schwinn; grandpop bent down a little to tug the line to the shutter. There was a picture of me posing with Col. Cole at the Memorial Tombstone and one of me shaking hands with the mayor after the parade for saving Mirabella. There were snapshots of me holding the inner tube before communion and blessing the hamster and sitting on a burro at Uncle Charlie's Golden Age death house and receiving the Second Place Chain. I hung the most of the negatives of Mirabella and me outside the movie. I must have taped a hundred photos in the three towers. I had tons of left-over pictures but no more time.

A whistle shrilled at the far end of the tunnel; Col. Cole whistling and galloping. I took off.

I escaped through the gym window. Willy arrived minutes later with blood on his muzzle and we sped back to Galápagos. I didn't think Col. Cole recognized me in the dark. Then I remembered the trash barrel with my darn address painted on it.

Kathy was still flat on her back. In a panicky rush, I set the motion picture camera at the end of the cot on its tripod and the battery spotlights on each side of the camera. I propped Kathy's head so she stared into the light. I hung my Kodak thirty-five with a hundred millimeter close-up lens and an automatic sixty second timer on a hook next to her head. I hung the second Kodak across from it.

After pulling up the ladder and locking the locks, I ordered Willy under the cot until I was finished. I addressed an envelope to the National Teen people and composed a letter and read it into the tape recorder.

"To Whom It Might Concern:

"Throughout all of Human History the Great Man has voyaged to new frontiers. I don't think

I'm a Great Man, necessarily. I'll let the experiment speak for me.

"I am a ninth grade student in junior high school. During my life, disguised as an ordinary boy, I've examined and torn down all the myths that mankind used to say were the way to live. The pyramids of the past lie mashed around my feet. With the help of my grandfather, I have erected a brand new pyramid, the pyramid of Spirit.

"In my experiment I will be testing the new pyramid with the magic words my grandfather got from Horace, King of Fireflies.

"My grandfather is sort of John the Baptist. Not that I'm a Jesus or anything. Actually if you want comparisons I'm more of a Job. To prove who I am, I will cure my sister.

"She's eight years old now but she was very little the day she got sick. I was sitting at the kitchen table building a balsa wood model of a Spad biplane. Kathy was playing tea party in the dining room. Her dolls sat around a card table with a centerpiece of plastic roses in a jelly jar. She politely asked them if they'd like more tea or graham crackers, if they were having a good time. She was really a great kid.

"I heard her start to cry. I discovered she'd pricked her finger on a plastic rose thorn. I smooched it to make it better. Kathy hushed and poured a second helping of tea all around.

"I didn't hear from Kathy for a long time. A tin teacup clattered to the floor. I was gluing rice paper to the plane and couldn't leave until it dried. Later, I found her staring at the dolls; it was sort of like she was imitating the dolls, who were staring back at her with painted on pupils.

"After that she hasn't shut her eyes. They're wide open day and night. She sleeps with them open, twenty-three hours and fifty-five minutes a day. She doesn't blink; she doesn't talk.

"The doctors mom hired said her pulse was weak and she breathed in deep and exhaled fast like sighs. Pop had three world famous faith healers pray over her. They decided she had been placed under Satan's worst spell and this particular type of curse was impossible to faith heal.

"I will cast out Kathy's demon! I will bury Satan under the snow! All the people in the U.S.A. who suffer trances will be cured! All the people in the galaxies of the universe! This is the greatest experiment in history!

"I will get this universe moving again! All people with blank expressions and all people who stare at the tube all day and all people who are sick of the world and don't bother to get out of bed will shout my name!

"I will set up the results tomorrow morning at the school with the other kids. The world will know who I am when the Fair opens at nine a.m."

I signed the letter and licked the envelope. On the governor's copy I added "P.S. I'm looking forward to lunch."

With one Kodak I snapped Kathy from all angles. I hung up the Kodak and set both Kodaks on automatic. After introducing myself to the tape recorder and giving age and location, I turned on the movie camera and lifted my vette keys from my pocket.

"It's now nine minutes before midnight," I informed the recorder, checking my watch. I swung the vette keys in front of Kathy's eyes. "Keep Up Your Spirits; Keep Up Your Spirits," I chanted at the one syllable per second suggested in *Hypnosis to Amaze Your Neighbors.*

At twelve thirty-five my right arm was sore so I switched to my left arm. A queer haze was descending over Kathy's eyes.

At twelve forty-five her eyes were halfway shut: either she was falling into a deeper trance or she was part way through a long blink. "Keep Up Your Spirits; Keep Up Your Spirits," I regulated by the tick of my watch.

At twelve fifty my left arm gave out and I switched on time to my right arm. Kathy's eyes were clamped shut. If she opened her eyes again, it would prove she was at least a little out of her trance. I could say she had blinked.

Excitement in my voice would mess up everything. To keep cool I concentrated on my lunch order, deciding on two minute steaks with toasted rye seed rolls, home fries and Dr. Pepper.

But an hour later I was still chanting and Kathy's eyes were still clamped. The film refills were running out; I couldn't swing the darn keys much longer; my voice was cracking.

It didn't make much sense to swing the keys anyway with her eyes shut. I repeated the magic words and prayed my voice wouldn't quit: "Keep Up Your Spirits; Keep Up Your Spirits."

A coyote's wail came from under the cot.

Kathy's blanket rippled up and down at her hips. It was so slight at first that I wasn't sure if it had moved at all. Her spurs jingled and suddenly her boots shot from under the bottom of the blanket! Each time I repeated the chant, they zipped further out.

Her hair was bleaching into platinum and rolling down over her shoulders. Kathy smiled for the first time in eons! She laughed and dimpled!

Her chests were budding. All of Kathy was blossoming in the rhythm of "Keep Up Your Spirits; Keep Up Your Spirits; Keep Up Your Spirits."

I wanted to clap my hands and shout the wonders of grandpop, but I couldn't break the slogan because she still didn't have her eyes open. Another problem was I couldn't chant much longer or she'd grow too big for the cot.

I flipped back the blanket to check on her underneath. Folded across her chests and attached behind at each shoulder were two transparent wings! "Ye Gods!" I yelled.

Willy crawled out snarling. Kathy jerked up, unfolded her wings and took off like a jet-propelled helicopter. She whammed blindly into the roof and ripped the tarpaulin and jolted the rafters. Leaping on the cot, Willy snapped at her while she flapped dizzily around the walls. He bit her wing. She hit a rafter and flopped back on the cot, screaming unsonically.

I tried to hang on to Willy and pet Kathy's hair. She'd break a wing and maybe ruin my chances if she kept on floundering around. But I couldn't calm her.

Undoing the locks, I tried to boot Willy out. Kathy sensed the air through the door and flew over my head. But she didn't make it out the door; she went through the roof and knocked off two beams with her wings. The walls crashed into the maze. One of Kathy's spurs tangled in the tarp and she flapped and screamed, trying to yank it loose.

"Sic her! Save her!" I ordered Willy. He lunged, but a wing smacked him down. She ripped out. Willy charged into blackness.

All I could see was Kathy's orange blinker zooming straight up and turning very small.

Twenty-One

THE cameras and recorder were in a heap of glass under the tarp. Since the judges only needed to know Kathy was cured, I erased the noise of what happened after I discovered her wings. At the end of the tape I concluded "If the winner isn't at home, wait for further instructions on where to send the lunch invite."

I packed all the gear and the shotgun in the tarp and let it down. Willy was mostly conscious, wandering lost in the ruined maze. He had no hard feelings about my kicks; if he did he'd have to be chained up. No animal was going to stop me now.

Kathy's ten gallon hat lay at the foot of the hickory. Snapping Willy on his leash, I gave him a sniff. If she got too weak to fly, Willy could track her across the fields and through the woods. We dodged from tree to tree. Kathy might have circled and flown in the front door of the house.

After searching all the rooms and the attic, we rushed around the front yard and checked the shrubbery.

I tried the back yard, sweeping my eyes through the branches. On the fifth sweep the corner of my eye caught a flash. We galloped to the edge of the yard. There was Kathy, perched halfway up the radio tower, blinking saffron, surrounded by red tower flashers.

She'd come back to me!

Even from that far I could see how she was shivering. I started to climb to her, but I thought and quit. She'd probably panic and knock me off the tower. I jumped down.

I'd never even held a gun before. Trying to remember how the Cisco Kid did it, I sighted at one of her glistening wings. Blam! I missed. The second barrel I aimed better. Blam! The universe went wild!

Kathy toppled off the tower. I moved my legs to run and catch her but discovered I was falling from the kickback. Willy's leash snagged in a maze log as he tried to get in position for a bite.

The curdlers went off; immediately the floodlights switched on and the night disappeared.

Fluttering, Kathy ditched in the snow next to me. Willy charged at her dragging his log and managed to snatch a mouthful of wing while Kathy clobbered him with her fists and free wing. I cooled Willy with the butt of the shotgun. I pulled him off of Kathy and bent down to look at her injury.

Her eyes were looking at me! The blast had jolted them open! "Hello Governor!" I yelled at the stars. She blinked her eyes to show me how happy she was that I got her all the way out of her trance. Her gun wound was just a swatch from her left wing tip. After I dabbed at it with my flannel shirt, the bleeding slowed up.

The curdler was piercing to the core of my brain. All over the neighborhood the other curdlers, fire sirens and burglar alarms were setting each other off. I had to escape the noise or my brain would have been roasted in decibels.

It wouldn't be long until mom and pop and Col. Cole got on my trail. If I survived until the contest opened, they wouldn't dare touch me: I'd be too famous.

Galápagos was the first place they'd look. I thought about cutting out in the vette, but the cops would spot it too easy. There was only the cellar. Mom and pop would think the cellar was locked and the curdler would be muffled. By dawn things would have quieted down and I could make a break for school and set up for the contest.

I wrapped Kathy's wing tip with my under-shirt and toted her into the house. With a candle, I lit a path across the long cellar, past the swimming pool to pop's work table. I planned to lay Kathy down there for a thorough inspection. Leaning Kathy against me, I shoved the stuff on the floor and grabbed a pile of *Sunday School Times* magazines to spread out for Kathy.

She didn't look like my little sister Kathy any more. Except for her sweet face she didn't, except for her dimple smile and her soft baby skin. All the rest had really changed. The cowgirl skirt was way too short for this Kathy. Around her gun belt where she used to have a tummy, there was nothing. Her Deputy Sheriff's badge stood way out.

With The Hand choking me, I gagged and must have turned purple. Kathy smiled and touched me lightly. The Hand let up and never returned.

"Can you talk now, Kathy?" She shook her head and I looked disappointed. She tried to cheer me up with her little girl tea party laugh.

"Do you hurt anywhere?"

She shook her head fast.

"Now we can bowl upstairs and go to the

196

flicks and take picnics in the spring! And I can teach you to read and write a heck of a lot better than you learned in nursery school! You can help out with my homework and maybe I'll even pass this year and you can take down notes during meditation period!" I blurted, embarrassed by the tears slopping down my cheek.

Kathy wrapped a wing around my waist and kissed my tears.

"We can rebuild Galápagos and live up there together and Friday nights I can take you to the church hops," I said. I tuned in pop's workshop radio that he built to hear evangelists from around the world. By music from the Voice of the Andes, Quito, Ecuador, I tried to teach Kathy to dance. She had good rhythm but no concentration.

After a while, we rested in the beach chaises next to the pool. I asked her if she could answer questions about herself and about life in general. She wrote her answers on the back of the *Sunday School Times.* "Kathy are you a messenger from King Firefly? Will you tell me how your blinker blinks cold light? About where fireflies are beckoning us?"

She wrinkled up her forehead and straightened her mouth. "WHAT THAT?" she wrote.

"Do you remember a cloud kingdom of bubble mountains and polka-dot umbrellas?"

She nodded.

"Where? When? What cloud?" I asked, leaning forward.

Kathy bent over her magazine and took a long while writing. "CAPTAIN CANGOROO," she wrote, smiling at me, expecting I'd be turned on with her writing ability.

I sank back in the chaise. "Kathy, could you give me advice?" I asked much later.

"WHAT THAT?"

"How should a guy find love with a girl?"

She opened her wings, grabbed me with them and almost pulled me out of the chaise. "But what if she doesn't have wings?" I asked over her shoulder, my spirits plummeting. "What motto would you give to support the human race?"

"MY WENGS" she wrote, making a silly face and fanning her wings.

"Be serious!"

But she wouldn't pay attention.

There was a rumble of cars overhead in the garage. The back door slammed. We heard mom's voice grumbling while other people stomped snow off their galoshes.

"An arm for an arm," Col. Cole's voice said.

"Let the police handle this," the chief's voice said.

Kathy blasted off! She crashed into the beach furniture and the diving board and the water filter pump. She collided with the candle. "Kathy you're on fire!" I screamed.

"He's in the cellar!" mom yelled from the kitchen. Clomp, clomp, clomp, lots of galoshes marched across the dining room rug.

With her eyes shut tight, Kathy rammed into the ping-pong table, the pinball machine, the billiard table, the jam preserve cupboard. Her wings whipped the pool into tidal waves. Once she rested under the stairs, her mouth open in a silent scream. I went to pet her and pat out her flames while she looked at me pleading.

Col. Cole ripped open the doors and boomed down the stairs. But he didn't get far: he locked into shock when he spotted Kathy. When Kathy saw he didn't have a dog, she opened her wings to embrace him. But Willy woofed upstairs.

Kathy closed her eyes again and flew off wobbly, dive-bombing straight into the pool. A huge wave snuffed the candle.

Col. Cole dashed up the stairs howling for help. In the dim light of the cellar window, I saw Kathy lying face down in the water. I reached her with the skimmer pole. Standing on the floating ping-pong table, I scrambled up the window well and dragged her after me.

With Kathy slung across my back, I ran as fast as I could. Halfway through the back yard, I caught my breath behind a tree trunk.

The lights flicked on through the house one

by one as mom searched for little Kathy. In the kitchen, Col. Cole mouthed into the telephone. Pop shut off the curdler and came out into the yard to say a few words to the cop that guarded the vette. He inched into the floodlights: "Kipper, aren't you out there somewhere? I know you must be confused about something, but I'm sure we can pray it out."

He was starting to say the same stuff to the dark at the front of the house when a battalion of fire trucks clanged down the block followed by the whooping of the Civilian Disaster Alert.

Hefting Kathy across one shoulder, I ran to the base of Galápagos and grabbed the tarp of experimental gear. Soon I was far enough back in the woods so I could hardly see the flashing lights.

It was slow going. I got hung up in a clump of wild raspberry bushes and needles stuck in my boots. I kicked them off. Remembering George Washington and winter at Valley Forge and patriots with rags on their feet, I ran on in my socks, across a field and through the muskrat stream and into more woods and past the willow trunk.

At the Sacred Hill, there were three miles to go. I footed it through Happy Farms without any trouble. The houses were black and sleeping. After all, daylight was Monday and the kids had to be in school and the dads at work.

Then it was only two miles to go and the going was easy. I followed a cross-country trail straight up out of the valley. My feet were bleeding a little, but I couldn't feel a thing.

At four forty-five I was at the towers. Since the judges wouldn't arrive for a few hours yet, I sat on the front steps to rest and watch. All over Happy Farms, curdlers and sirens were setting each other off. Fire engines, cops and Disaster Squads hustled from one alarm to the other, flinging searchlights in the air. The cops stopped at the curbs and bathrobed people left their houses for them to investigate inside. Helicopters hovered over the woods dropping purple flares. One pilot thought he spotted something and dumped tear gas cans into a group of volunteers. A mess of penlites paraded out of a bus—the Echelon boys and Gardenia girls, led by Reverend Hocheisen. In a while the penlites fanned out on the hillsides.

It was fun watching them make a fuss especially when I remembered in a few hours they'd be shouting my praises.

With Kathy and the gear, I hurried through the hole in the gym window. The army didn't bother to come inside; I guess because they didn't figure I could have run so far so fast.

I tiptoed past Col. Cole's dark office and rode the elevator to the top. The new exhibition hall glowed with reflections from the hundreds of white-clothed tables sparkling in the moonbeams. Dangling over it all was a banner: "National Junior High School Teen Scholar Contest."

I picked the closest table to the door so that the judges would notice Kathy first thing. After spreading out my cameras and the recorder, I eased Kathy down next to them. I untied the shirt from her wing tip and peered at it by moonlight. It was clotted and seemed o.k. I stripped off her frozen outfit and wrapped her in tablecloths. After jogging around the hall a few laps to get circulation back in my feet, I climbed up and snuggled under Kathy's tablecloths.

I saw my victory parade with me at the head and my fans hooraying behind me. Cowgirl Kathy circled overhead while below Mirabella wiggled in joy, waving the American flag and cheering "Keep Up Your Spirits!" Hunnicut dashed ahead to shove a path through the frantic crowds. A Shop L fife and drum corps set the march beat. Onward we streamed down the main hall. Col. Cole got in step and clashed the cymbals as we laughed into the sunshine. Haloed in sunlight, I shouted a sermon, "Now we declare war on the enemies of life! Now join hands for Spirit!"

Kathy rustled her wings. Her blinker was covered. I lit a match so she could see me.

Smiling, she thanked me for saving her life. She kissed my bleeding hand and yanked the raspberry stickers with her teeth. We smooched until the match flickered out. I explained I couldn't light another one because of the soldiers.

Kathy wrapped her warm wings around me and I rested my head on her chests. In wonderful dreams, we slept together on the squeaky table, holding each other like we used to in her bed. When the hall began to gray, Kathy threw off her clothes and soared to the skylight where she saw her first sunrise. She laughed sweetly each time the sky turned from purple to bright pink and an explosion of yellow. Gliding gracefully around the hall, she showed me the healing in her wing tip.

At nine o'clock sharp, Col. Cole arrived with his bandaged arm to open the hall for the setting up of projects. Kathy flew over and hugged him in her wings. I tried to explain to Col. Cole how that was my exhibit who used to be entranced but now was wonderfully alive, but he looked at me with horror in his mouth and pushed her off and ran to the elevator, bawling for the army.

It took the authorities hours to bring Kathy down. Of course, if they'd left their German Shepherds in the K-9 Corps Kennel, she would have swooped into their arms. They were going to shoot her at the suggestion of my hysterical mom who said it was just a naked insect now. But a tender-hearted soldier wouldn't do it either. This upset Col. Cole because there were kids lined up with projects who saw Kathy naked.

Finally the city fuzz sirened out the express-way with long suicide nets. But Kathy was a very successful mutation. She flew over the nets and was too speedy for their dope darts. Before somebody stabbed me in the rear with a needle, I dodged around yelling the magic words of the crusade.

I guess they tricked her. The newspapers say they got her about lunch time and penned her in the SPCA.

My *People* cover was years early, according to my schedule. I also made it on *Newsweek* and *Reader's Digest.* The *Digest* never had a person on the cover before me.

Newsweek and others lined up behind Kathy, saying she's "an oracle from beyond our Rational-Scientific Milieu." They were upset because she wouldn't answer questions and they suggested it was because of the violence of our Age.

I dictated a letter to *Newsweek* pointing out if I were sprung from the clink I could get Kathy to write any answers they wanted. *Newsweek* ran my letter in capital letters alongside of an editorial blasting the skeptics.

There are a lot of these dopes around. They are led by *Time.* "Kathy, or 'K' as she or it is now labeled, is an example of the Moral and Genetic Degeneracy of the Twentieth Century. America has come to the end of its rope in ballyhooing the finale of the human race," *Time* said.

"Past ages have been granted grandiose titles to describe their achievements: The Golden Age of Greece, The Renaissance, The Age of Reason. Historians will have little to say about our age. For us alone is reserved: The Age of the Punk.

"There is nothing new about Punks. They have always been counted a sizeable part of the census of the Human Race. But formerly they inhabited the kitchens of inns, the haystacks of stables and the back rooms of brothels. They lived and died in obscurity. It remained for our democratic age to raise the Punk from the kitchen, haystack and brothel and deify him. In our pop-culture it seems the Punk sells. His image advertises an array of deodorants, rock records, books and motion pictures. Mass Media underscored this point recently in the case of a young man who ruined his baby sister. Since his name is already a household word, we will not further glorify him by repeating it.

"There is nothing brilliant about this fellow. His looks are less than endearing: a gigantic body topped by a long nose and a crop of pimples. His personality affords us less to admire, let alone worship. His report cards indicate below average grades; his extra-curricular record gives us a mediocre trombone player, a cross-

205

country runner who never raced and an aspirant to student office. His main occupation was driving a super-powered sports car. In his relationship to his parents, he was loudmouthed and obnoxious, an all too frequent phenomenon of our time. He retired from his loving home to a tree fort where he whiled away his hours, attempting to seduce girls. He didn't even possess the gumption to join others his age in a meaningful demonstration against some of the real social evils of our time.

"Somewhere along the line, this fellow got it into his head that he wanted to be famous. He was encouraged in this daydream by the rosy propaganda of the tax-supported National Teen Scholar Foundation, which offers fame and fortune without guidance to its would-be Einsteins, and Frosts.

"One night, while his parents attended the viewing for his Uncle Charles, he kidnapped his sister from her crib. Although she had been incurably ill for several years, he exposed her to the rigors of below freezing weather and bundled her off to his apartment laboratory where he experimented. It remains to be seen just what occurred that evening. A full-scale investigation by federal authorities is underway. The Punk is not talking, insisting on a fantasy about magic words his alcoholic grandfather—a failed poet—taught him. His sister, who should be declared legally dead if the Supreme Court ever comes out of session, has been replaced by a mute monster with wings and vastly exaggerated sexual characteristics. The facts will probably always remain a mystery, especially the facts of the monster's blinker light.

"What is even more mysterious is the mass hysteria surrounding this Punk. College students riot almost daily for the Punk and his monster. Normal citizens, including many keystones of American community life, seem to have lost their wits. The President has been unable to control his own daughter, Tania, who has formed a liaison with the Punk.

"Historians will surely seize upon this incident and afford us our just accolades. Enter the Age of the Punk."

What a laugh! I had the chief cancel my subscription.

I didn't get chow with the governor. The cheap judges mailed me an Honorable Mention for effort, said my experiment classified as more spiritual than intellectual.

Sure King Firefly helped me out with his words. But just because I got a hand doesn't mean I shouldn't win—Moses, Elijah, Lazarus, St. Paul, St. Theresa, you name it, they got help from outside. Nobody accused *them* of cheating.

The judges voted first prize to some kid who pasted together a working model of the Paricutin volcano. Jeez! I'll bet his dad built it!

Tania agrees that Kathy is the end of the human race as we know it. Kathy's true identity will be written by later ages with more info. The best we can do is to retreat into the past through Anthropology. She thinks the BWFL fossil throws a lot of light on the problem.

Tania is waging a write-in campaign to save Kathy. She argues that Kathy belongs at MIT where she can get love and cerebral understanding. Otherwise she thinks Kathy will shrivel away in a month or so. She says future ages won't forgive us if we lose the Link with them.

Future ages! If Kathy dies they'll have *me* to reckon with, now!

Tania makes sure they're taking care of me in here. She's hired the best lawyers. But the trouble is the lawyers can't proceed until somebody figures out what the charge is.

Mirabella ran away from home and the F.B.I. says she's a Missing Person. There's a rumor around that she was last seen swimming off into the sunset at Atlantic City. Nice girl! She reverts to a coelacanth just when I need her to organize the school for the spirit crusade.

I can see Tania now, double-parking her Jaguar. This is her third visit today. She wears tight shorts with her shirt tails tied in front to show off her belly button. Secret Service guys cross the street beside her, hefting boxes of complexion soap.